D1462311

MIND-HOLD

Also by Wilanne Schneider Belden

Mind-Call
The Rescue of Ranor

HARCOURT BRACE JOVANOVICH, PUBLISHERS

San Diego   New York   London

MIND-HOLD

Wilanne Schneider Belden

Requests for permission to make copies
of any part of the work should be mailed to:
Permissions, Harcourt Brace Jovanovich, Publishers,
Orlando, Florida 32887.

"Shine on Harvest Moon," music by W. Jack Norworth,
lyrics by Nora Bayes and W. Jack Norworth.
Originally written for the score of Ziegfeld Follies.
Copyright 1908, Remick Music Corporation.

"In the Evening by the Moonlight,"
music and lyrics by James Bland.
Copyright 1878 by James Bland.

Library of Congress Cataloging-in-Publication Data
Belden, Wilanne Schneider.
Mind-hold.
Summary: In the aftermath of a devastating earthquake,
twelve-year-old Carson is responsible for his own
survival and that of his spoiled younger sister, who
despises him for partially sharing the mental powers that make her so dangerous.
[1. Extrasensory perception—Fiction. 2. Survival—
Fiction. 3. Brothers and sisters—Fiction] I. Title.
PZ7.B38882Mk 1987 [Fic] 86-19370
ISBN 0-15-254280-9

Designed by Michael Farmer
Printed in the United States of America
First edition
A B C D E

To Robert, whose constant caring assistance with all the technical aspects has made my life and my work a thousand times easier—even though he never reads a word I write. With love.

MIND-HOLD

1

When the earthquake was over, Carson discovered himself alive. Despite his complete entombment, his first reaction was not terror but relief. He was surrounded by what had been the walls, ceiling, and roof of his room, but he *felt* as if an enormous weight, which had grown heavier daily since he was four years old, had been lifted from his body. Considering his situation, this made no sense, but Carson accepted his lightheartedness as gratitude for having survived—so far. He tried to find out more about how—and where—he was.

He seemed largely unharmed, aside from a few cuts and bruises and a bloody lip. He licked the blood off, spat, and checked to be sure he had all his teeth. The answer to "How?" was "OK." Now, "Where?"

He could move fairly freely, and he sensed that he was in a confined yet open space. Two beams of orange light, almost opaque with dust motes, illuminated tiny circles in a squarish darkness. He turned his head away and closed his eyes. He needed all the dark-adjustment he could get. In a moment or two, he could make out that he was half lying under his worktable. It was a large rectangular construction of solid oak his great-grandfather had crafted years ago. Solid, massive, scarred, and ugly, the table almost had been sent off to Goodwill. Carson had talked his mother into letting him have it for a workbench. His models and constructions wouldn't harm it any. He grinned. Nothing could, even an earthquake.

He set about the job of extricating himself from the destruction of his home with a euphoria he could not remember ever having felt. He moved slowly and carefully, aware of the precariousness of the debris, and shifted each lump of plaster, downed stud, and broken object with precise care. It took him nearly an hour, but he was successful in wriggling out without so disturbing the mass that it further entrapped him.

Though Carson did not consider his accomplishment particularly noteworthy, the likelihood of it was on the order of locating a particular grain of sand on a hundred yards of beach at high tide. Carson knew that other people did not have his relationship to the forces in the areas around their bodies, but he'd never thought of his external sensory network as unique. *Unique* was a word applied, in the Bleeker family, exclusively to Caryl, his distinctly peculiar younger sister.

Carson did not like Caryl. A more unlikable child than

she would have been difficult to find. So long as he didn't make an issue of it, his parents never asked him to like her, nor did they suggest he should feel guilty or ashamed of his dislike.

He finally traced his feeling of elation to a source.

Carson Daffyd Bleeker, age almost-thirteen, earthquake victim, sat in the orange sunlight on a mound of rubble covering his worktable and realized that his sister probably hadn't lived through the quake. Even if she had, the time he'd taken to free himself might well have proven fatal to her. He knew he should be sorry and ashamed of his reaction, but he was not. His personal millstone had been split in two, like the earth, and had dropped off his neck. Simple problems like survival he could dismiss, if he didn't have to spend the rest of his life baby-sitting a kid who worked magic.

Caryl was nine and had demonstrated her peculiarities even before she could smile, an activity in which she rarely indulged from then on.

Carson felt as if the last nine years had been an endless procession of days in which he dragged himself along an ever-deepening rut—the rut in which he lived chained to a child who actively hated him. With reason, he had to admit. Nobody else could control Caryl. Carson could.

No one, least of all Carson, knew why, but she couldn't do her tricks—although they were much, much more than tricks—if he said, "No!" and meant it. He had often spent days, weeks, in constant, exhausting mental battles with Caryl. As she had grown older and stronger, so had he. So far.

He heard a sound. Caryl crying.

To Carson's everlasting credit, while the idea of leaving her there did pass through his mind, he dismissed it as it arrived. But for several reasons, he did not leap to his feet instantly and begin to search. Had someone demanded a moment by moment account of his thoughts and actions during the next hour, Carson could have explained his few minutes of inactivity with the physical reasons: the precariousness of his position, the need to determine Caryl's location, the time he must take to plan what to do. They were all true. He need never have told anyone but himself the primary one. Five minutes of freedom weren't much, and the burden was a good deal heavier than those most fully mature adults had to shoulder. The galled places in his mind and spirit hurt desperately as he picked up the ends of his psychological chains and locked them in place again. He could keep from screaming only by breathing with whole-minded intensity.

The condition of the air made this an unwise choice. He coughed and choked, and the cut on his lip began bleeding again. He did not care.

"Caryl," he called, "be quiet. Listen, or I can't help you."

She screamed, of course. Fury, not pain. Carson could tell. His instructions had received the response he expected. Why Caryl hadn't caught on that Carson often told her to do the opposite of what he wanted, he could not fathom. Caryl had a perfectly good mind.

The sounds led him to her.

Carson worked slowly and carefully for over an hour. He paused to rest often. Otherwise, when Caryl was free, she would be stronger than he. Should his hold on her slip, he might be in considerable danger. No one else was available to blame for the situation, and Caryl would try to take out her anger and fear and pain on him. She always did. Everything in the world was directly and specifically involved with Caryl. If something outside her control went

4

wrong, she had to punish someone for it. Carson was the closest.

Disgusted with himself, Carson stopped. The situation had robbed him of his own ability to reason.

Carson sat down and felt out to Caryl below, trapped but no more physically damaged than he. Yes, she could now get out by herself, even if he did nothing more to help her. Getting out would use up her stored power and solve one of his problems—for a while.

"Too tired. Got to rest. Back in a few minutes," he told her. "I'm going to see if I can find something to eat."

Caryl's scream of frustrated impatience and utter hatred nearly deafened him. He stuck his raw fingers into his ears and teetered carefully across the rubble to where the kitchen had been.

His luck changed slightly for the better. By applying force at precisely the correct angle, Carson was able to slide the entire roof structure that now covered the battered but unbowed refrigerator over the roof of the garage, some four feet lower.

The loud rumble it made effectively covered the noise Caryl caused by exploding her remaining covering of rubble and the firm mattress that, doubtless, she had folded over her body to save her life.

Not that it was an actual explosion. Nevertheless, at nine years old, Caryl's ability—magical, telekinetic, psionic, or whatever it was—was great enough, particularly fueled by her present emotional frenzy, to remove what still trapped her. Carson could only hope he had judged correctly.

He gulped milk from the carton and watched to see if his sister would scramble out on her own immediately. If she could, he'd done too much for her. He found a hand towel in the debris, shook and slapped it, and wiped off his face. The resulting mess sent him to the fridge again for a couple of ice cubes. All the time he was cleaning himself up, he kept half an eye out for movement from the new crater. None. Caryl had even stopped screaming and telling him off. Carson was so used to both that he no longer noticed either except as indexes of Caryl's emotional state. Years ago, in self-preservation, he'd stopped paying attention to her words.

When ten minutes had passed, he called, "I've got the fridge open."

Part of Caryl's anger had been at Carson's ability to locate food and eat, while she could not. The idea that anyone could come before her invariably infuriated her. Carson could eat, and she must go without? Unthinkable!

A couple of hard-boiled eggs rocked a bit in the door-rack. One of them lifted an inch or so out of its niche, then clicked back in. Deliberately, Carson picked it up, peeled it, and ate it.

Caryl's scream this time was tens of decibels less in volume, though no less in intensity. Her throat sounded raw, and she coughed.

Carson began to hurt. He squelched the pain with every erg of energy he had left. Survival for both of them depended upon his not giving in. He could not, must not, be forced back into the habits of before. Caryl could always, often by intention, break him to do her will, serve her need, just by needing help desperately enough—her kind of help, the "me first, me only," pattern of her life. He stood, the hand holding the towel shaking so hard that the terry cloth flapped, and denied her.

Caryl began to cry—not to yell or scream or express her selfish egotism—just cry like a normal, frightened, nine-year-old girl.

Yesterday, Carson would have rushed over to help her, to make her feel better. Today, he began throwing rubble out of the ex-kitchen, making of each piece a hammer of sound to cover his sister's sobs.

Despite his best efforts, his attention centered on Caryl. What he was doing took little or none of his ultra-senses. Thus, he felt Caryl's situation. His mind pictured her safest moves, what and where she could and could not—at her weight, size, and strength—slide over or under, move, lean against, or step upon, to make a safe passage from the unbalanced mess she had more thoroughly scrambled. Once in a while Caryl seemed able to follow his mind pictures almost as if he were sending them. This shadow-thought almost let him black out his ultra-awareness of her movements. Not quite. For all his dislike, Carson knew he had no real choice. Caryl was his responsibility. If she got some good out of what he couldn't stop himself from doing, so much the better. She would never mention it.

Almost ten minutes later Caryl climbed out of her hole. Stumbling and falling, crawling at last, she made her way over to him. *She should get an Oscar for that performance,* Carson thought. He knew she wasn't *that* bad off.

"I hate you," she half whispered, half sobbed. "Go away!"

Something snapped in Carson's mind—almost a physical sensation.

"That's too bad," he said very softly. "Really too bad. Who's going to take care of you if I leave?"

"I can take care of myself," Caryl grated. *"Go away!"*

The narrow slash in Carson's inner space widened. "You're fairly bright," he said. "Look around. How do you think you're going to make it alone?"

Caryl stared at him, then turned slowly and began to take in the unbelievable reality around them. A strange whine—a sort of keening—began in the back of her throat.

Carson ignored it. "You think you might have caused the quake, I suppose, but you didn't. You couldn't. You're not powerful enough. I couldn't, either, and I wouldn't have, and I certainly wouldn't have let you. It happened, and you have nobody to blame, because I won't take it anymore. No one else around here seems to be alive. If they are, they're so trapped that they can't get out. Mom's in that hospital you put her in. No matter how soon Dad starts, he won't be able to get here for days. Not with all this."

Caryl started to interrupt with protest.

"Shut up!" Carson ordered. Exercising his mental control over Caryl's behavior, he held onto her vocal apparatus. She silenced.

Sure she couldn't speak, Carson relaxed his hold. Caryl's keen arose, and Carson had the feeling she wasn't aware she was making a sound.

"I'm going, all right," he shouted, demanding her attention. "Just as soon as I can find a few things, like a knife and some matches and something to wear and eat. You can go with me, or you can stay here and take your chances."

He began throwing rubble again, searching for anything he could use. The thuds and clanks and clatters punctuated his sentences.

"If you go with me, I swear I'll leave you behind—and be glad to—if I ever again have to listen to one more word of hate or blame, or one more sentence of your bad-mouthing. I've had it—" he gestured—"up to here. I'm drowning in your selfishness. I need all my energy to stay alive."

He looked over, to see Caryl's agonized, terror-stricken expression. She wasn't listening, and she had to. He stepped closer. For the first time in his life, Carson hit his sister. He slapped her briskly across the face, stinging and sharp but not hard enough to bruise her or to break the skin. The life came back into her eyes. And the hatred.

"Say one word, Caryl, and I'll hit you again. As hard as I have to, to make you shut up and *listen*." Part of her terror, he knew, was caused by whatever he'd done to prevent her from speaking. If he did it again, she'd be unable to pay attention. He would have no other option than to slap her into awareness.

Caryl said a word—a word she wasn't supposed to know— and Carson hit her so hard that he split her lip.

He expected her usual flurry of hands and nails and knees. Caryl was skinny but all muscles, stronger than she had any right to be. Carson had been taught not to fight back, not to hurt her, only to control her in such a way that she did not hurt him. This time, the widening space in his feelings made him hope she'd try it.

She didn't. An entirely different expression—one of such shock and stunned surprise that Carson laughed—replaced her usual self-involved truculence. She stood rigid.

Carson took advantage of her stillness. "I'll get you as far as the nearest people who'll take you—and I won't tell them why they shouldn't—and that's all I'll do. Cross me, fight me, tell me off, order me around, blame me—one more time, and you're on your own."

He turned away, ducked, and let the chunk of concrete she'd thrown at him pass over his head.

"You know you can't hurt me that way, Caryl. Why waste the energy? You're going to need all you've got."

He moved beyond the range of her kicking feet, pulled more kitchen towels out of the mess, and sat down to wrap them around his feet.

9

"Thank you," he said softly. "For the first time in my life, I'm free of you, and you did it all by yourself."

Caryl extricated a couple of knives from the rubble and threw them at him. Carson caught them easily, one in each hand. "Thanks again. Now, how about some matches?"

The moment the word left his mouth, he regretted it. He knew exactly how Caryl would react. He needed the matches, and he knew how long and with what effort he would work unaided to find them. But matches could be a weapon, and she'd use it.

In a moment, a book of matches floated into Caryl's hand. She smirked.

Reaching into himself for whatever it was that had stopped her from speaking, he applied it to her movements. Pack open, one hand ready to pull off a match and strike it, Caryl froze. The look of terror came back, and she struggled. He tightened his hold until her fingers began to go white.

With unknowing confidence, Carson strode through the rubble and took the matches out of his sister's hand. "Thank you again."

He released her.

His sense of her intention to mind-move warned him. Probably, she'd try to ignite the whole book in his hand. This time, he said, "No!" and meant it.

"Use your nose—" Carson paused. He wanted to call her "stupid," but if he wouldn't allow her to call him names, he must set an example she could not turn back on him. He continued, "—Caryl. Take a deep breath. What do you smell? That's gas. All the gas mains are broken. Do you really think you could keep yourself from being burned if it all went up?"

Caryl's pale face scowled at him. Her mouth made movements he lip-read as "I hate you."

Carson shook his head.

Caryl had no energy left. White and drained, she slumped into the mess. No tears dripped down her face, but she sat and cried silently.

Carson examined his inner awareness of Caryl. He always knew how much power she had and whether she intended to use it, but Carson spent several seconds making sure. Someday she might learn to fool him. Not today. She was safe, or he was, or they were, for at least an hour or two. He ignored her and got to work.

2

When Caryl dragged herself to her feet and began to act as if she planned to accompany him, Carson had to ignore her as though his life depended upon it. He realized it might. Caryl's "poor little me" act could melt the heart of a glacier in Antarctica at midwinter. He continued to make up a pack, selecting only what was absolutely necessary. He found himself packing her toothbrush with his and tossed it down angrily. If Caryl wanted a toothbrush, she could get it herself.

He glanced her way several times, curious to see what she'd pack. A small sense of surprise and grudging approval made him shake his head. Caryl was choosing only what she had to have. No furry bears or rock collection. No dress-up dresses. No books.

A few minutes later he was startled to hear her voice.

"Are you . . ." She stopped. "Are you taking soap?" she asked. Her tone of voice was neutral.

"Yes," he answered. "You take toothpaste."

"OK," she said. "Throw it over."

"Please," Carson required.

She did not speak for a full minute.

"Please."

He threw it and the toothbrush, then her comb. He'd operate on the reward system, he thought. When she did what he wanted her to without being unpleasant, he'd do a little more for her than she asked. Otherwise, nothing.

He waited. "Well?" he asked.

"Thank you," Caryl said.

"You're welcome. Anything else here in the bathroom that you want?"

The silence this time lasted somewhat longer. Carson continued to sort through rubble. He grinned to himself. Caryl couldn't get what she wanted by mind-moving it; she was too tired. She'd have to walk over here, and she didn't want to. She'd never had to learn to ask for things courteously, but she was learning that she could scream, "Frog!" until she turned green, and he still wouldn't jump. She was debating the options.

"Yes, please," Caryl said. "If the antiseptic's not broken, and some Band-Aids. My feet are cut."

Carson started to stand up to go help her, but sank back. *Ah-ah-ah! Smart, that kid.* He'd nearly bitten.

He sopped a towel in the toilet. The bowl was broken, but the tank remained in one piece and fairly free of debris. "Catch," he said. "Wash off with this. I'll see what I can come up with."

"Thank you," Caryl said. She sounded disappointed but determined.

He grinned again. He'd already located the iodine, and it wasn't broken, but he wondered if he could find the zephrin intact, too. It didn't sting, so Caryl would be more likely to use it. She might avoid infection. Right. Here it was.

He took off his towel wrappings and saw to his own feet first, then his other cuts. He capped the bottle and tossed it to her. "Catch. I'll find the bandages next."

Carson could feel his sister's simmering anger begin again. He should have seen to her needs before his own. Nothing and no one was as important as she, and she'd pay him back but good for not remembering it.

Before she had time to work up a real snit, he cautioned, "Think first, Caryl. If you use up any more energy being angry at me, you may get left behind."

Caryl looked daggers at him, but Carson could feel fear overlay her anger, and she began to calm down.

Score one for both of us. We might just make it, Carson thought. He had little real belief, but this was a step in the right direction. For the first time in her life, Caryl had controlled herself. However, she was undoubtedly adding to her mental list. She'd find a time when she could pay him back for all the unforgivable things he'd done—with usurious interest.

Maybe he could get her sense of self-preservation to work for him.

"If I can't walk, I can't take care of you."

Caryl's simmer died. She must be thinking it over.

Now, he had to clear that up. She mustn't be able to say he'd promised he *would* take care of her. "If you don't take care of yourself properly and get infected through sheer stupidity, I'll leave you. And I'll also know when or if you can't make it on your own. Don't count on being carried or babied just because you want to be." He considered telling her that from here on, she'd follow his orders or suffer the consequences. But she'd never suffered a consequence in her life, and he knew she wouldn't understand.

"Fix my feet yourself," Caryl shot back at him in her "I am the master—you are my slave" voice.

Carson had always resented that tone of command, but in the past he had followed her orders. This time he laughed. It surprised him as much as it did Caryl.

"So I'm wrong, whatever I do? No way, sister dear. You're responsible for your own feet. Take care of them properly or find out what it means to suffer the consequences. If I have to do one thing for you that you can do for yourself, I'll leave you. Remember it."

"You're awful!" she said.

In comparison with her usual diatribes, her remark was so mild that Carson laughed again. "Not nearly as awful as you are, but I'm learning fast. After all, I have the first-prize, blue-ribbon, A-number-one awful to teach me how."

"Yes, I am, aren't I?" Caryl agreed. She smirked.

"And you're the only person on earth who'd be proud of it," Carson rejoined.

Caryl threw a pebble at him—by hand—in response. It came nowhere near him, and Carson decided she deserved that much release for her feelings, so he ignored it.

Carson expected a problem when he chose their direction of travel—Caryl's automatic disagreement with anything he suggested. He was in no mood to play her games today. She could follow or not as she liked. No one was nearby to see anything Caryl might do, no one to frighten or anger, no one to harm.

He went as directly as he could to the middle of the school playground—the closest large, open space he could think of. The school, built to the newest earthquake standards, was far less damaged than other structures he passed. This fact registered as peculiar in Carson's extra sense. The school was part of the expensive new housing development in which they lived—had lived. All of it was built on filled land, which was notoriously unsafe in earthquake country.

He did not turn to see whether Caryl followed him. He was still split inside. On one side, he hoped she'd follow, so he wouldn't have to go get her. On the other, he hoped she wouldn't, so he could be free of her. Had he been paying attention to his thoughts or feelings, he would have found himself fairly well-balanced between the two extremes. At the moment the dangers in his physical surroundings were more than enough to keep him busy.

He walked out to the pitcher's mound and sat down. His extra sense informed him that something big was building underground to the northwest, something so powerful and all-consuming that it was as much as he could do not to curl up in a ball and give in to mindless terror. He knew it must be an even more world-changing earthquake. But the first one hadn't been able to harm him, so he refused to let this second one take him over before it even occurred.

He sat on filled land, but he trusted his extra senses to let him know where the land would split, so he could be on a part that wouldn't.

As he waited, his attention centered within himself, Carson realized why he had so deeply disliked their new house. All the time this quake had been building he had somehow known it, but he had been unable to assign a reason for his apprehension.

Carson had been glad when Dad took Mother to the hospital for alcoholics, well out of the area, glad Mother had at last agreed she needed help. Because of his inexplicable apprehension, he had been deeply relieved that neither of his parents were to be home over the weekend. He had practically begged his father to stop and visit with his parents on the way back. Daffyd Bleeker had expressed some reservations, but finally agreed. It would be silly to pass right through the little town in which his family lived and not stop to see them. Carson knew his father needed a few days away from Caryl. Everyone did.

Carson never previously had accused his sister of making his mother's illness worse, but no one who knew the family and the situation could have been unaware that Elisha Bleeker had been drinking more and more. And when she was drunk, she could shut out the realities of her impossible daughter. If Carson hated his sister, he did so for this reason. If Carson accepted the responsibility for controlling his sister, he did it for his mother. He loved his mother very much, in a bumbling, wordless way no one but his father understood. He sat on the mound and kicked at the hard-rubber pitcher's line and was glad his mother was alive and might have a chance to get well.

About his father, Carson felt less protective. To a degree, he resented his father's work because it kept him away from home so much of the time. When he wasn't home, Carson had the full responsibility for Caryl. The resentment was countered by the realization that Daffyd Bleeker was a successful man, at the top of his profession. Among other things, his excellent earnings enabled the family to have Caryl tutored at home after regular school hours, when Carson could be there. If Caryl had been required to go to school . . . Carson hated to consider what would have happened the first time someone failed to realize Caryl's supremacy.

In these last moments before the second major quake, Carson made a decision. He would, somehow, take Caryl so far away that she would never get back. And without having to face life with her unnatural daughter, Mother would be able to grow strong again. Mother would never know he had done it, but he didn't need her thanks. Maybe one day he could get back to see her—without Caryl.

He had a purpose in life, a general plan, and a direction. He would go east far enough to be out of the earthquake damage, then north. Their West Coast relatives lived to the south. If it was ever discovered that he and Caryl had escaped unharmed from the ruins of their house, they would be sought to the south. Therefore, east, north, and as far as possible. It would take some doing. Adults felt it their responsibility to tell unaccompanied children what to do and to see to it, with force if necessary, that they did it. But if he let Caryl slip occasionally, Carson knew he could get the two of them thrown out of almost anywhere by almost anybody. He started to refine his plans.

Caryl arrived, making much of her sore feet, when the quake was almost ready to begin.

Carson stood up. "Wait here," he said.

He walked the playground quickly, feeling the forces beneath, evaluating the probabilities. There was the weak spot. This part of the land would rise, that part fall. If they were *here,* they would roll into the split. If *here,* they would tumble away from it. He went back for his pack.

"Come with me, if you want to. I'm going over there," he said to Caryl. He pointed.

Later he realized that Caryl talked the entire time. He heard—or attended to—not a single word she said. He picked up his pack and stumbled to his chosen position. Walking was as difficult for him as if the earth already shook. He fell, curled around his pack, and waited. Had Carson acted in any normal manner, Caryl probably would have died. She was so confused and curious about her brother's peculiar behavior that she followed him into left field, dragging her pack behind her.

The center of the baseball diamond split. Half of it tilted almost forty-five degrees and dumped the top layer of soil into a crevice. The earth on the home-plate side of the field rose and shifted north almost four feet. The gap slammed shut with a deafening roar and incalculable force.

3

When the earth stabilized, Caryl was a trembling ball of terror, reduced to silence. Carson picked himself up, stamped, and smiled. His sister raised her head a little and stared at him. He realized she thought he'd lost his mind.

"It's over. There'll be a lot of little aftershocks, for months probably. But all the energy is released. You can trust the earth again."

Carson waited until Caryl uncurled and sat up.

He almost said, "Let's go," as he would have to anyone else, but stopped in time. "I'm going now. You may do as you like." He slung his pack over his shoulder and started east.

"You can't leave me here alone," Caryl protested, sniveling. Carson wished he couldn't hear her.

"Why not?" he asked. He continued to walk. He did not look back.

"Wait up," Caryl called.

Carson did not slacken his pace.

"Please!" she called.

Was that a note of desperation in her voice? Carson smiled. Well, so far, being awful was working. It ought to. It had worked on him for nine years.

But she had said, "Please," so he stopped.

"Carson, I'm hungry," Caryl said as she shuffled up to him.

Her powers of recovery surprised him.

"So am I." He kept his voice reasonable and quiet. "Where do you suggest we find something to eat?" He didn't think she had a suggestion, but if he asked her, she might not ask him.

"The school garden," she answered. "You told me about it, about the carrots and radishes and things. I like raw vegetables."

Justifiably, Carson was surprised that Caryl should remember something she had seen only from the car window and had, as was her wont, disparaged. He turned in the direction she pointed. Nothing recognizable as the garden showed, but there might be undamaged vegetables in the tumbled earth.

"Good idea," he agreed. He shifted his course, expecting her to come along. In a few paces, he discovered she hadn't. "Well, if you're not hungry," he said.

"I thought of it, you get it," she said. She smirked.

"No go. Get your own. Otherwise when I have an idea later, I won't let you in on it."

He did not wait to see the results of that statement. Behind him he could feel her reach out for the vegetables. He let her. She'd use up more of her power harmlessly. Knowing Caryl, she'd get far more than she could carry, and he could benefit. She tried to pelt him with dirt and leaves as the vegetables flew by, but missed completely, as usual.

Carson harvested his future meals by hand, braided the tops together, and hung them around his neck. He had quite a haul, and they'd be with him tonight. He ate a turnip, a carrot, and tried a raw beet. Not all that bad. Hm. Onions. He made another braid. Onions helped the taste of almost anything you couldn't put chocolate in.

"Mine don't have any dirt on them," Caryl flaunted.

"I don't have to carry mine in my hands," he returned.

Caryl started to "poor little me," and Carson started back for his pack, eating a not-very-dirty radish.

The vegetables were a good idea, Carson thought, because they helped him to feel less thirsty. So far, all he'd found to drink were a couple of dented cans of tomato juice and a plastic bottle of distilled water, which he'd hung on his belt. It was a nuisance, but he knew he'd need the contents.

As if thinking about thirst had conveyed the idea to Caryl, she began to complain about it. Carson grinned. Some of the radishes were hot.

"Where should we get some water?" he asked. He found that keeping the nastiness out of his voice was difficult, but he managed to speak with equally irritating sweet reason. Being nice to Caryl resulted in her getting the upper hand.

"In the swimming pool, dummy."

"In the swimming pool, who?"

"Dummy!"

Carson hit her. Not hard—or not too hard.

Caryl wailed.

"Who?"

Caryl looked around. Usually when she made this sound, people came running.

Nobody came.

"Who?" Carson asked again.

"You!" she screeched.

"I don't answer to put-downs anymore," he said. "I thought I made that clear. Good-bye."

He almost stumbled over her huge pile of vegetables. How did she think she could carry all that? She'd found some summer squash and cucumbers, too. He shoved a couple of each into his pockets and started in the direction of the swimming pool.

It had split and crumbled, but one whole corner had tilted in such a way that it held water. Carson was pleased to see how clean the water was. It smelled a little of chlorine, but he doubted that it'd harm them any. Caryl would complain, but she complained about everything. He lay down and drank. Just in time, he caught the feeling and kept Caryl from dumping him head over heels into the water and running off with his braids of vegetables.

"Stupidity is no excuse," he said as he got up. "Would you really want to drink it after I'd wallowed around in it?"

Caryl pouted. "It's all your fault," she said. "You made me mad."

Carson thought several words he couldn't say. He settled for "Nuts! Nobody *made* you anything. You got mad all by yourself. Stop trying to blame other people—me, for instance—for what you do. Believe it or not, the world does not revolve around you—nor does it, nor I, give a tinker's dam what will make you mad or happy or anything else. I'm not your slave or your servant. Be courteous, be pleasant, or be damned." He was pleased with that last turn of phrase.

"You hit me when I said a bad word," Caryl said. "What're you going to do about you? You know Mama cries whenever you swear."

She knew exactly how to hurt him, and reveled in her ability. Reference to his mother's pain if he used even the mildest bad language stung Carson. He must not let Caryl know she had scored. "I was not swearing or using bad language," he said. "I was explaining what you could do." It wasn't much of a defense, but Caryl didn't know how to react when calling up the specter of Mother to make Carson punish himself hadn't worked.

Caryl smelled chlorine and demanded Carson's bottle of good water. He pretended not to hear her. At last, she held her nose ostentatiously while she drank. He grinned to himself. He'd been mistaken. She couldn't complain much. Drinking the swimming pool water was her idea.

Carson was relatively proud of himself for one thing: if Caryl wanted to go on conversing with him, she had to trot along at his side. He led her as east as he could manage, and every block was one less to go.

They spent the night in the ruins of a house. Carson did not point out that the ruins doubtless covered dead bodies, but he was careful to select a house where he saw no such evidence. His choice of shelter proved fortunate. The people who lived here had camping equipment that he and Caryl pulled out of the rubble. When they went on tomorrow, they'd be a lot better equipped. Sleeping bags,

24

for one thing. After Caryl was in hers, asleep, Carson sat up for a while and thought.

They had not come very far today. After the winds began, it was difficult to see their way. They were in so much danger from flying debris that he'd had to let Caryl use her ability to keep herself from being hit. Carson protected himself automatically from all such incidents in the world around him, and it seemed to cause him no energy-drain, but Caryl tired quickly. Carson had been forced to locate a place to hole up before his sister collapsed altogether.

They had seen several people during their hike, but no one paid any attention to them. The degree of shock and the totality of the devastation appeared to have driven any concern for others out of the minds of the few survivors. Carson felt relatively safe from interference with his plan.

Carson awoke with first light, hearing something. A radio! The slight shifts during the night must have turned it on. He searched almost frantically. If he could locate it, he might have information on the areas of greatest destruction. He had refused to think about it, but their parents might not have escaped unharmed. He believed the hospital and the tiny town in which his father's parents lived were well out of the danger zone, but . . .

He found the small transistor radio at last, plugged the earphone into his left ear, and turned the volume low. He'd hear what he needed to.

When they went on after breakfast, Carson was properly shod. A pair of hiking boots he'd found fit him well enough if he put on three pairs of socks. His sore feet were much less painful and might begin to heal. He insisted Caryl carry another pair of boots. They were slightly too long, but about the right width. She'd been growing so fast this year that Carson hoped she could wear the boots when her tennies fell apart. They were bound to soon, if the footing kept on being so bad. Who knew if they'd find anything better?

He kept to the hills as much as possible, for in them the damage had been less, but he always worked east and north. By late morning, he judged, they would come to the long central valley between the two slender mountain ranges. He was afraid they wouldn't make much time or distance today, either. The valley was located directly over the main faultline. He—they—might be forced to go south.

4

The wind continued all the following day, but Carson made himself go on. Until he stood looking down into the water-filled valley, he did not realize he had been hurrying. The aftermath of the tidal wave halted him completely. Had he actually thought he might find the valley dry? He knew how narrow the land-bridge was between the ocean and this faultline. He had to have known that when the mountain barrier broke, the ocean waters poured through the gap and filled low areas such as this—particularly this—with new arms of the sea. He had come as fast as he could. Why? Getting here quickly had made no difference in the amount of water or in the difficulty of getting to the other side.

Or had it?

Somewhat to the south of his vantage point was a new section of the freeway. The bridge that had won the architectural contest last year still arced from one side of the valley to the other, high above the flood and destruction. The curve was no longer perfect, but the gap in the center was almost unnoticeable from here. Carson felt rather than saw the twist of the nearer section. He must get closer. Perhaps . . .

He chose a resting place where he could sit and look at the bridge. The bases of its supports were now below the churning water in the valley, and they had not been designed to withstand such forces. Carson had no field glasses, but his distance sight was excellent. Sections of the concrete span appeared to have buckled, but he believed the reinforcing steel still held. He could make his way across it if he had to crawl with his eyes shut.

Caryl could make it, too. Dad and Carson had built her a complicated and expensive construction in the backyard: ladders and platforms and rope bridges, tubes and poles and lattices, a marvelous place where she'd spent hours swinging and sliding and climbing and crawling.

Had built. Had spent. The backyard construction was kindling.

Sheltered from the wind by a huge rock, Carson was fairly comfortable as he sat overlooking the valley and the bridge. He almost thought—hoped?—he'd lost his companion, but Caryl struggled up to him.

"Carson," Caryl said.

He didn't know whether to feel happy or sad, so settled for feeling nothing. "Here," he said.

"Why didn't you wait for me?"

"If I had, we'd still be there," he answered. "You followed the trail well. You may thank me for leaving it. Otherwise, if you fall behind again, I won't."

"Thank you, Carson," Caryl grated through her teeth.

He'd heard diabolical imprecations on the Friday Night Late Show with less intensity of hate in them.

"I'm going on," he said. "The longer that water pounds at the bridge supports, the less likely we can get across. Come on, if you want to."

"Why do we have to go across the bridge?" Caryl asked. "Why didn't we stay where Daddy knew we were?"

"*You* do not have to go anywhere," Carson responded. He had no intention of explaining his reasons to Caryl, now or ever. "You may go back to what's left of the house, if there hasn't been a fire, and wait until Daddy gets there, if he can get there at all."

"Oh," said Caryl. She pointed. "There are people at the end of the bridge. Why can't we stay with them? Things aren't so bad here."

"Stay with them if you want to. I'm going across."

"Why? *Why*, Carson?"

"Because I want to," he said.

"That's not an answer."

"It's all the answer I'm going to give you."

She simmered, and Carson wondered what tactic she would try next.

"Carson!" Caryl wailed. "You had a chance to rest. I'm tired."

"So wait. It's your choice. I'll leave a trail. You can follow me the way you did this morning. If you wait too long, the bridge may fall, and you won't be able to cross it. Then, when you get into other kinds of trouble, you'll have only yourself to blame." He referred, and she knew it, to the several instances in which he had been aware she was making magic.

"I didn't do it when anyone could see me," Caryl protested. "Only to make it easier to get over things and to keep the wind from blowing things into me."

Carson looked down at her. "You may live to grow up," he said. He slung his pack over his shoulders and took off down the hillside. "Though I doubt it," he finished when he was out of earshot.

He picked his way along the slope, trying to keep a windbreak between himself and the fierce, cold wind. Caryl cried and complained, but she came on behind him. He chose a route she could follow, not sure whether he resented the need to take longer, less difficult ways when he had a choice. Doing so might lose a little time, but it saved strength. He did not help his sister in any other way. If she made it, she'd have to do it on her own. Caryl had spent her entire life putting off on others—principally Carson—any duty, any activity she did not fancy. If she succeeded in accomplishing this, the worst necessity of her life so far, never again could she require help by saying, "I can't."

This abrupt re-direction of his behavior bothered Carson. He must constantly be aware of his habits and prevent himself from returning to the position of Caryl's personal slave. Never again could he do for her what she could do for herself—not if he was to retain enough strength to prevent her from using her powers in some way that would jeopardize their lives.

When they arrived near the bridge, the group of people Caryl had spotted stood between them and the beginning of the span.

Carson retreated behind the nearest screen of rubble

and opened his last can of tomato juice. Caryl was too tired to speak, for which he was grateful. They shared the drink and ate limp raw vegetables.

Caryl wanted to go out and throw herself on the mercy of the people. Carson said she could if she wanted to, but he'd keep her from talking about him. He was going across the bridge.

Caryl became angry again. Anger gave Caryl strength. Carson decided to use it. He stood up, shrugged his pack into place, and went on. He knew she'd be yelling something at him he didn't want to hear, so he hummed under his breath and tried to remember the words to a song— any song—he could sing loudly enough to drown her out. The angry wind would blow Caryl's words and his song away from the people, who were, in any case, not paying attention to anything except their own attempt to cross the bridge.

The people were stringing themselves together with ropes. Carson walked quietly around the knot of men and started across the span.

For a miracle, Caryl chose this time to be very quiet and to follow her brother with movements as self-effacing as his. The two of them were almost to the gap in the center of the bridge when the first of the group spied them.

Shouts and screams and orders having no effect upon the children, one of the men, with the rest of them holding a rope, started out after them.

Carson reached the broken place. As he had suspected, it was not empty. The steel reinforcing bars, twisted into demon-bent pretzels, led from one end of the roadway to the other. He knelt and tested each one by reaching over and taking hold of it, then pulling with all his might. Three were unsafe—loose at one end or the other. Four more were solidly anchored. He sat up, slid over the edge, and started across. He used the lower two steel rods as footway, the upper two as handhold. He was so used to ignoring screaming, demanding, ordering voices that he paid no attention to the man's shouts until after they'd stopped.

Had the gap been wider, Carson could not have made it. The force of the wind and the peculiarity of his path required every dyne of his strength. Arriving on the other side safely, he kicked loose several chunks of broken concrete until he found one that would hold him. Then he crawled onto the other lip of the bridge. In the entire operation, he had not opened his eyes once. He did so now.

The man was holding Caryl by the arm and preventing her from following.

Carson grinned. Caryl's would-be rescuer could have done nothing more certain to prevent his intention from being carried out. If Caryl was told she couldn't, she mustn't, she wouldn't, she reacted by proving she could, must, and would.

This time Caryl was smart. She untied the safety line from around the man and retied it around herself. The long rope had several knots. Another knot untied itself. The free end flipped across the gap.

Carson caught it. He tied it off to a solidly anchored rod which, in breaking some four or five feet from the edge, had reacted by bending upward.

Openmouthed and horrified, the man discovered what had happened. Caryl said something to him, and the man dropped her arm. He turned, dropped to his belly, and crawled back toward the end of the distorted roadway.

Caryl freed her end of the rope, tied her pack onto it, and threw it. Carson hauled it in. As soon as he had untied the pack, the rope returned to Caryl like a flying snake. It tied itself around Caryl's waist. She sat down on the edge of the broken bridge, hooked a knee over a rod, tucked the toe of that foot securely behind the other knee, grabbed a higher rod, and began to pull herself along the strange path. She did not pause, and she did not look down.

When she reached his edge, Carson lay flat and pulled her onto the concrete. "Well done," he said.

Caryl smiled. A real smile, not a smirk or a grimace. "Thank you," she whispered.

The roar of the wind would have made a shout impossible to hear, but Carson knew Caryl said real thanks in so soft a voice that he wouldn't have heard her in a closed room.

The bridge began to sway and bob.

Carson erupted to his feet, grabbed Caryl's hand, and pulled her along. Caryl ran hard, and they made it to land seconds before the bridge collapsed behind them. Jolted off their feet, bruised and scraped but intact, they rolled and scrabbled off the roadway onto the grass at the side.

Caryl sat up. "My pack!" she yelled. She shut her eyes and concentrated. In a moment, the pack soared through the air and dumped itself at her side. Caryl lay flat, her face white. "That was hard," she said. She opened her eyes. "Carson, can we stay here for a while?"

He nodded. He could not have answered if his life had depended upon it. Reaction had set in, and Carson was terrified. Beside him, Caryl began to shake, then to sob, and, in a moment, Carson thought she was going to throw up. Breathing hard, he moved away, so if she did, he wouldn't. He was too close to throwing up as it was.

Once the worst of the crisis passed and the shaking and sweating stopped, reason returned. He was safe. They were safe. They still had their packs. They'd never again see the people over there across the gap. Even if the man had stayed on the span and thus had seen Caryl's pack rise, he could do nothing about it. Carson hoped the man had made it back to safety in time.

He stood up. The part of the bridge on this side was essentially gone. The supports had given way, and the roadway, wrenched to the side, had broken off. The other end of the bridge still stuck out like a lopped branch, though shorter than before. The man—Carson recognized him by his brilliant yellow jacket—was standing safely on the far end of the bridge, looking this way.

Carson waved. If he had worried about the man, how much more worried the man must be about them. He had, after all, only tried to prevent them from killing themselves. Carson yanked his sister up to stand beside him. "Wave," he directed.

She was too weary and sick to protest, so she waved once.

The man waved back.

Carson untied the rope from Caryl's waist, tied her pack onto it, and wrapped it around his shoulders so he could tow it behind him. "Hold it up a little," he ordered Caryl, "or you'll wear it dirty as well as wet."

"I can't, Carson," she said.

He didn't respond, just grabbed the back of her jacket and half shoved, half helped her to slog along beside him. The pack rose an inch or two, enough to make it easier to pull. Funny, what Caryl couldn't do.

They must move now, before the chill factor of that glacial wind turned them both to statues. They had to find shelter before they gave out.

Over the crest of the hill lay the highway construction

yard. The prefabricated metal shed was twisted but still upright, and a big bulldozer had careened through the wire fence, so they could get to the shed.

"Down there," Carson shouted into Caryl's ear. "Inside."

Caryl nodded. She turned to shout to him. "I can make it by myself," she said. She took the rope out of his hand and started toward shelter.

Carson nearly fell over. Of all the astounding happenings in the last two days, this single sentence was the most unexpected. He rotated to free the rope and stared after her. When his tongue got dry, he remembered to shut his mouth.

They were lucky again. A watchman must have used the shed, for there were a cot, a campstove, and minimal supplies. A five-gallon bottle of water had been thrown out of its spindly stand, but it had fallen onto the cot and been wedged almost upright, losing little of its contents. Carson set up the stand and reinserted the bottle. Caryl drank and drank.

Carson dug out his toothbrush and the toothpaste. He filled a tin cup with water and went outside to brush and rinse away the taste in his mouth. Much active swishing freed him of the sensation that he'd been chewing on rusty nails. Stale fear tasted terrible.

His watch told him it was only a little after four, but he was hungry and exhausted. Food would help. Caryl actually helped to set up the campstove and locate an unused can of Sterno. Carson opened a big can of stew, heated it, and they ate supper.

Their truce lasted through the next day, which Carson considered the personal dispensation of Divine Providence. Thick smog swirled down the valley and swarmed over the heights. Masses of oily smoke and ash and acrid fumes forced them to cover the window as best they could and to remain in the leaky shelter of the shed. To save the batteries, Carson listened only to the hourly news summaries on the little radio. So far as he could determine, his parents and grandparents were safe.

That afternoon, it rained. Carson found a deck of cards and taught Caryl to play gin rummy. She continued to be pleasant-tempered.

They had fallen asleep with the sunset the first night, but neither of them could get to sleep tonight. Caryl, increasingly high-strung from the combination of her emotions and her overstimulation, reverted to normal. Carson, tired, worried, cold, and uncomfortable, almost was reduced to anything to shut her up, to giving in so he would not have to fight her. Almost. He retreated instead to the pretense of sleep. She disturbed him several times by poking or kicking, thinking that she was waking him. At last, he had to threaten.

"Caryl, if you don't shut up and leave me alone, I can stop you, you know. I've had all I'm going to take. One more time, and I'll paralyze you."

She reacted with absolute stillness, body and voice.

Finally she slept, and Carson, who had been afraid he'd never be allowed to sleep again, was so relieved that he dropped into dreams without knowing they were not reality.

5

The next morning was the worst one of Carson's life. When Caryl woke from her nightmares, she was almost hysterical. She wanted Daddy. She even wanted Mother. Everything was Carson's fault. She tried, unsuccessfully, as always, to harm him. Today, he was certain she was trying to kill him by every means at her command. He felt utterly miserable himself and wanted their parents as desperately as she did. Finally he gathered his things and went outside. He climbed into a big earth-moving machine and increased the barrier around himself to include the Cat, so she couldn't damage it by throwing rocks. He locked the door. Now she couldn't get at him. Let her rage as much as she liked. He was safe.

Frankly, he didn't care what happened to her, as long as she left him alone.

He cried for a while, alone on the high seat in the sunlight. While it didn't seem to help much, it made him feel a great deal better. He slept, dreamlessly this time, and woke feeling both stronger and calmer. The Cat had a radio, a luxury Carson would not have expected. He located a classical music station that interspersed the constant news bulletins with short, soothing pieces—Bach chorales, Debussy nocturnes, and the like—and listened for an hour or so. The music, as it always did, filled an empty space inside him, and he was able to listen to the news reports with less frantic fear. Still no mention of the area in which Dad and Mother were, but much about places closer to their former home. He began to hope that all might be well. Not only was he glad that, in all likelihood, Dad and Mother and Dad's parents were all right. A small part of his mind kept hoping that since his father could not get through to where they'd been, Dad didn't know they were no longer there. Carson did not let himself think about how his parents would be worrying, suffering, not knowing their children had lived through the quake—and not knowing their present whereabouts.

No sound came from the hut, but Carson knew Caryl was inside. He always knew her location in space. He hoped she'd been able to get some good sleep, too. Maybe she'd feel a little better and not be so poisonous. He was in no mood to ruin his sense of peace, so he did not go near the shed. Instead he hitched on his pack and the canteen he'd filled earlier and set off down the road. He'd try to find someone to come and get Caryl.

The idea of taking her where she'd never again be a problem to Mother was a fool's dream, he recognized at last. He couldn't really take care of himself, much less be responsible for Caryl. They'd be out of food in a couple of days, even with the camping dehydrates they'd looted and the canned beans and stew in the shed. They could be a hundred miles from nowhere, although he didn't think so. Ten miles might be as dangerous. He didn't think Caryl could walk another ten miles.

Whatever had made him believe he could carry out his plan to remove Caryl from Mother's life?

Frightened, futile thoughts slowed his pace. He dragged along the road. Hungry, he did not want to eat. Lonely, he remembered stories about strangers and wondered if he could trust anyone he might encounter.

Would he meet anyone? This was a new road, unfinished. With the quake and the need for every ablebodied person to help find survivors, nobody would bother to come out to the construction site, probably for weeks.

He stopped. Of course people would come! Bulldozers and other kinds of earthmovers and haulers were in that yard. They'd be needed—if anyone could find a way across the gap. Surely, farther south, someone would find a way. Could he get one of the big machines started?

Carson almost dropped his pack in order to run faster, but he decided against it. He settled for a fast, steady pace, and returned to the construction yard in an hour—half the time of his trip away from it. The sun seemed to shine more brightly. The world had lost its aura of gloom. He had a goal, a possibility, and he felt better—so much better that when Caryl came out to meet him, crying and complaining about his having deserted poor little her, he merely walked around her and went out to his Caterpillar.

He checked every vehicle in the yard. All required keys. Keys. Where had he seen keys?

"This what you want?" Caryl's sneaky, triumphant voice inquired. She dangled a bunch of keys temptingly in the air before his face.

Carson knew better than to reach for them. She'd played this game too often and always won.

Not this time. Carson got mad. Mentally he reached out and grabbed Caryl savagely. Not even a moan would he allow her. When she put those keys in his outstretched hand, he'd release her body. Until she did, she could stay in stasis, probably hurting as the muscles cramped and spasmed. He waited.

When the keys dropped onto the ground, he merely flicked his hand. He waited again.

At last, the keys rose slowly and clinked into his hand. He closed it firmly. Caryl could never wrest something away from him with her mind, not if he knew she might and really held on to it.

"Thank you, Caryl," he said pleasantly. He released her.

She fell to the ground, wailing in her "I'm being tortured" tone. Carson ignored her.

He took only a moment to locate the key to his big Cat. It was not the largest of the machines, but it looked as if it could do a lot of earth-moving. Yet it was not so large that it couldn't travel down narrow roads and through constricted spaces. Too, it proved to have a full tank of diesel fuel, and he could strap two of the barrels somewhere, if he could manage to lift them.

He shortened the headstrap on the huge, sound-deadening earmuffs, put them on, and started the engine. The sense of power was heady. He spent another twenty minutes learning the controls. While no unusual strength was necessary, and Carson was both sturdy and strong for his age, he had neither the required height nor reach. He had to figure out methods by which he could manage. Kneeling on the seat or standing up, depending on what he was doing, seemed to be adequate. When he decided he was as ready as he was going to be, he turned his attention to the matter of fuel again.

His laugh of surprise could not be heard over the roar of the engine, but it made him feel even better. Manage to lift the barrels, for Pete's sake! What was the machine *for?* He maneuvered for a while, finally scooped up two barrels in the curved blade, and tipped it horizontal. They might not stay unless tied down, and he had nothing to . . . Oh, yes, he did.

He turned off the Cat and climbed down.

Caryl was inside the shack. She pulled her head out from under the pillow when he came in. Caryl hated any noise she did not make herself, and she reminded him of it. He stared past her until she ran down. Then he said, "May I borrow the rope you got at the bridge?"

"No!" Caryl said automatically.

"I need it to tie the fuel barrels onto the blade, so I can take them with us."

"With you," Caryl said. "And you're going to have to figure out something else. I want my rope."

In answer, Carson stepped over and yanked the blanket off the cot. He could cut it into strips. While it would not be as strong, it might work, and he had no interest in fighting with Caryl over the rope.

She screamed and grabbed for the blanket. "I need it. It's cold at night."

"One or the other," Carson said. He felt and acted both calm and determined.

She wanted both. She must have both. How dared he want something important to her?

41

In the end, she let him take the rope.

Carson was alert for his sister's attempt to retrieve her possession while he was working the Cat. He stopped her. She screamed. He did not hear her. While he wore the ear-protectors, he could hear nothing.

As he steered his machine slowly and carefully along the road, Carson sang at the top of his lungs. He was having the time of his life. Since babyhood, Carson had loved all kinds of machinery, the bigger and more mobile the better. To have control of this land leviathan made him feel twenty years old and twenty feet tall.

At about four in the afternoon, a jeep bucketed toward him. He stopped the Cat and waited. The driver pulled the vehicle to a stop beside the Cat, and the four men inside stared at him with expressions of stupefaction.

Carson cut his explanations to a minimum and got down from his throne with disappointment. He had no reason to believe they would allow him to continue to drive, not with an experienced operator waiting to take over, but he had hoped. After all, if he did drive, it would mean another piece of equipment could be put into service. The moment they found out his sister was back at the equipment yard, they insisted he return with them to get her.

Caryl was not waiting. She had started down the road after him and had actually walked a couple of miles. She lay in a tiny patch of shade, her face as white as death. Each cheek had carefully drawn tear-marks like aerial surveys of river deltas.

One of the men jumped out with Carson and picked Caryl up. She cuddled her head into his shoulder, turned her face against it, and ignored her brother.

Carson sighed. It would start again. Poor little Caryl. He knew from all-too-sad experience that they would never believe he had planned to take her with him, and she had refused to come. He said nothing. The men's icy anger at his callous lack of concern for his poor little sister was clear.

The only redeeming result of the incident was that they decided he could drive a machine. They needed every one of them; he had demonstrated clearly he could do the job. Caryl would go in the jeep with the driver, who would drive it back only because the biggest machine was not useable.

"You'll need the blade," the man who'd made the decision said. "We'll put the fuel in the jeep."

Night came on, and Carson turned on the powerful lights. He concentrated on driving, a difficult task in the darkness. The hazards ahead on the broken roadway could make problems he had no intention of attempting to surmount. His was the only machine that did not have to stop, back up, have help from one of the others, or in some way cause a delay. The men noticed this at last, and swung their machines in behind his. Where he led, they could drive their big beasts. The controls of the dozer Carson drove became extensions of his senses. He strained muscles by having to reach so far, by being in such awkward positions so much of the time. But these sensations were mild irritants he noted somewhere below the level of consciousness. He and the earthmover were a single entity. He provided the brain and the directions; it supplied the power and mobility.

Earthmovers do not go rapidly. The ten miles to the end of the construction area, to a place far less devastated than any Carson had passed, took over an hour. Carson enjoyed every minute of it and wished it were longer.

When he pulled onto the highway toward the group of

lights indicating an emergency camp, he didn't feel particularly tired. He turned into the space indicated by a man waving a flashlight, and turned off the engine. He did not want to get out. No one could see him in the darkness, so he patted the wheel and whispered thanks to the bulldozer as if it were a trusted animal.

Someone stepped up to the side. "Kurt?"

Carson climbed down. "My name's Carson Bleeker," he said. "My sister's in the jeep with one of the men. We couldn't bring the biggest earthmover. It has a broken axle."

The man stared down at him. Carson, although big-boned and well-muscled, was short for his years. "You mean you drove that dozer from the site?"

Carson nodded.

The man's flashlight beam swept up and down and came back to rest on the boy's face. Carson shut his eyes. When the man lowered the beam, Carson opened his eyes and smiled. "It was fun," he said. "I've always wanted to. It's easy."

"Holy Jesus, Mary, and Joseph," the man intoned. Carson had a feeling he meant it. "A kid. How old are you?"

"I'll be thirteen next month," Carson replied.

Apparently the man ran out of words. He shook his head slowly from side to side.

When all the machines were in place, Carson found himself the center of a group of adults who all seemed to have exactly the same reaction.

"Believe it or not," explained one of the other drivers, "we let the kid lead. He never had to stop or back or—hell!—anything. He'd drop the blade, push something out of the way, and go on. Like playing follow the leader where the leader does all the work." The man turned to Carson. "How'd you do it, kid?"

44

Another voice asked, "You sure you never drove one of them Cats before?"

A third voice broke in. "An' where would he do that?"

"Well, I thought he might live on a farm and be used to tractors or something like that."

Carson was trying to figure out an answer and welcomed the not-quite-argument as a delay. But now they all stared at him.

"No, I didn't live on a farm. And I haven't ever driven anything before—even a car. But I love machines. I've studied all about them. My dad's an engineer, and he's taught me a lot." Carson was careful not to tell a direct lie, but he was uncomfortable with what he'd said. An engineer his father certainly was, but his field of expertise was civil engineering. His work involved the engineering aspects of the design and construction of huge structures. Carson hoped the men wouldn't inquire further.

"Fer Pete's sake, we're here, the kid helped, whyn't ya shut up an' let 'im get some food?" another voice said.

"Food!" "Yeah!" "Thanks, kid," and other remarks broke the circle as the men's attentions shifted.

The man who had spoken up for him put his arm around Carson's shoulders. He spoke quietly into the boy's ear. "Name's Kurt," he said. "Kid, your sister talked since we got into the jeep. I know now y' meant what y' said about askin' her t' come with ya."

Carson didn't know what to reply. Simple self-preservation made him come out with, "I had to leave her there. Not for good, just to get help. My mom's in a hospital; my dad took her there Thursday. He stopped to see my grandparents on the way back. When the quake came, we had to get away from the broken gas mains. I've been trying to find somebody who'd help me with Caryl. It's hard. She's—she's not like anybody else."

"Kee-rist! Y' kin say that again! Nobody could be as bad as she says you are—except yer mom and yer dad and everybody else in the world. I'd say she's th' one oughta be in a hospital.

"Look, kid. We owe ya. Somethin', anyway, fer drivin' th' dozer. We'll try 'n' find somebody'll take y' in 'til y' kin get aholda yer dad."

"Thanks," Carson said. "Thanks a lot."

Tiredness swept over him, and he staggered.

"Jees, kid, yer done in. Here. Siddown. I'll get y' somethin' t' eat."

6

Carson woke late, warm in his sleeping bag. The camp appeared deserted. He looked around, nonplussed. *Boy,* he thought, *I must really have been tired.* He half remembered dreams of driving a gigantic earthmover. Pleasant dreams.

He stretched. Several muscles ached, and he was hungry enough to eat weeds. He pulled himself out of the bag, put on his boots, and made a beeline for the portable outhouse.

When he came out, a man called to him. "Hey, Carson."

He called, "Hi," and ran over.

"Name's Walt. I'm the cook—among other things—but

that'll do for now. Got breakfast for you, if you don't mind starting on cold cereal."

Carson grinned. "Anything, as long as there's lots of it."

Walt waved toward the long table. "Take any seat."

Carson shoveled in three bowlsful of what his mother termed "packaged air" and his father called "soggies" before Walt brought him a plate of fried Spam and over-easy eggs and a huge pile of buttered bread. He ate everything.

"Think you can make it through to lunch—a couple of hours?"

Carson nodded. "Thanks a lot."

"No problem."

Carson wished Walt hadn't used that word. He'd been doing his best to ignore his problem. He took a deep breath, stood up, and said, "Where's my sister?"

"Over there in a car. But, ah, Carson, before you go let her out . . ."

Carson's heart made contact with his boot-soles. He sat down again. "She's been trouble," he said.

Walt nodded. "Got some of the guys yelling, 'Witch!' "

Carson didn't want the details. "How come she's in a car?"

"Oh, everybody isn't running scared. Jim's got three kids of his own. When she started throwing things, he just grabbed her up, walloped her bottom good, and threw her in his car. It's got a special lock to keep kids in. I guess she hasn't figured out how it works."

Carson stared at the Formica tabletop. Well, so much for finding somebody who'd take Caryl. Not that he'd have let that happen. Ten hours' sleep, a good meal, and his determination had returned. He had to get Caryl out of here, farther north and east. "We'd better leave before the crew gets back," he said. "I'll go pack up."

48

"Ah, Carson?"

"Um-hm."

"Somebody passed a hat for you. Thanks for helping last night." Walt held out a thick stack of bills, mostly ones, but enough for bus fare or train tickets, if he could get to a station.

He took it. "Also for getting Caryl out of here as soon as possible?"

Walt nodded. "You don't do things like she does, do you?"

Carson shook his head. "Nope. Caryl's the mind-mover in the family."

"Speaking of family, you trying to get to yours?"

Carson settled for "Yeah." He stuffed the bills into his pocket and got up. "We sure can use the money. Thank everybody for me, please."

He started back for his pack. Walt followed him. "Look, Carson, I got another message for you. A couple of the guys said they, ah, didn't understand yesterday when they met you. They said to tell you, 'Sorry.' "

Carson stopped dead and looked up at Walt. Nobody had ever apologized for treating him like dirt because of poor little Caryl. "That's . . . Tell them it's OK."

"You got a worse job than we do, in a way," Walt mused. "Hope you get home soon—and that your folks are OK."

"They weren't in the quake," Carson said. "I've been listening on the radio. I think they're all right."

"Not what I meant. Well, yes, it is, but the sooner you get home, the sooner you get shut of her."

Carson shook his head. "That's not the way it works."

He could almost feel Walt's eyes tunneling into his back as he got his things.

The inside of the car was a disaster area. An enclosed

earthquake couldn't have done more damage. Carson lost his temper completely. "Caryl," he shouted, overpowering her screams and demands, "you don't get out of there until you fix what you've ruined."

She sat back. "I can't," she yelled.

"If you did it, you can undo it."

Caryl's expression was her customary truculent smirk. "No, I can't. And I won't. That man spanked me."

"Good thing." Carson turned to walk away.

"Carson!" Caryl screamed. "Let me out!"

He just shook his head.

He had to wait for over an hour, checking the progress of Caryl's careless repairs, before he felt the condition of the car was adequate. She couldn't entirely repair the damage, but what she could do, she finally did. *I'll get the man's name and address and send him the money to have it fixed right,* Carson decided. Maybe he could figure out a way to let Dad know about it without giving away where he and Caryl were. Not much chance.

He opened the door of the car. Caryl tried to scratch his eyes and kick his shins as she exited. Carson ignored her. "Get your things packed. They've thrown us out, thanks to you."

"I won't go. I'm tired. You go to the nearest town and call Daddy's office. They'll know where he is. Tell him to come get me."

"No," Carson said. "You have two choices. Come with me or stay here and end up being burned as a witch."

"You're just trying to scare me. I'm not a witch."

"Neither were the people who got burned as witches in Salem," Carson retorted. "They got scared to death."

Caryl went white. "You mean it, don't you?"

Carson nodded.

Screaming her rage, Caryl rushed across the campsite and grabbed her things. She ran back, pack spilling, and threw the sack and sleeping bag at him. "You do it!"

"No." Carson looked at his watch. "I leave here in exactly fifteen minutes. If you're ready, you can come with me. If not, you're on your own." He turned away and went back to the cook-trailer. Walt, busy with lunch preparations, looked up from the counter.

"Walt, I don't like to ask for anything else, but could you spare a couple of sandwiches and some water? And a map, or directions to the nearest town where there's a railroad?"

"Got lunch all ready for you," Walt said. "In the sack. And I've got something better. If you can drive a Cat, you can drive a jeep. Take ours." He wiped his hands on his apron and came over to Carson. "The road north's OK. First town's named Clarion. I drew you a map on the sack. Leave the jeep here, in the Highway Department parking lot." He pulled a pencil out of his curly hair and added some lines to the map. "Train station's three blocks over and two up."

"You'd trust me with the jeep?"

"Any kid who hasn't done away with a sister like her can sure be trusted with a jeep," Walt said.

"But—but I could just steal it."

"Not for long. Heard of the Highway Patrol?" Walt grinned. "But I don't think you would. I saw what you made her do to Jim's car—and how you crawled in and got the information off the registration. You'll do, Carson."

Not being able to cry was often a blessing. Carson had to swallow several times before he could speak, but that wasn't as obvious as tears pouring down his face would have been. "Thanks, Walt. You won't get in trouble?"

"Nah. Another one of my jobs is security. Besides, they need the jeep in town. This way, nobody has to take time off to drive it in."

Driving a jeep wasn't all that difficult. Carson knew about gears, the shift had a diagram on it, and by sitting forward, he could push the pedals. Carson told Caryl not to bother him and to sit still. The roadway was not entirely undamaged, and if she did anything to distract him, they might crash. "You'd get hurt a lot worse than I would," he warned her. The jeep had only one seat belt, and it was for the driver.

Caryl sat fairly still, but her mouth opened in half a mile. For the next hour, she complained without pause. Carson ignored her, as he'd had to do all his life, and they pulled up in the parking lot just before noon.

Carson got out, put on his pack, and snatched the food sack away from Caryl. Otherwise, he'd have no lunch. She'd eaten hers and planned to keep his for later. After telling her where he was going, he started for the train station. They were back in civilization, and Carson knew exactly how Caryl would react. He hadn't left the lot by the time he heard her "I'm being tortured" scream. Quite a lot of people came running. Carson plodded on.

The station seemed solid with people. Carson took a deep breath and plunged into the crowd. He used the rest room, washing down to his waist—hair included—in the basin, scrubbing the fur off his teeth, and finally taking off his shoes, rolling up his jeans, and washing up to his knees. The men who came in paid little attention, for the most part. Those who stared got Carson's best imitation of Caryl's normal expression, and he was left alone. He wondered how soon Caryl would get here. She would, of course. In her present state, she'd discover they wanted her to do something she didn't want to do, tell them off—or worse, and he'd let her—and they'd let her go, gladly.

He ate his sandwich and decided to buy two tickets for the first town to the east from which a rail line still led north, then north as far as he could get on the money he had. A bus would be cheaper, but the train station was the only place he'd mentioned to Caryl. He couldn't leave her, though he kept hoping maybe she wouldn't show.

She ran in, silent and frightened, as he was standing in line.

Should he ask somebody where the bus station was? He decided against it. Several places on the highway had been difficult to get through, even in the jeep, and he wasn't sure the buses were still running. The number of people in the train station made him believe the trains were operating normally. Better stick where he was.

He put an arm around Caryl and let her lean against him. When she stopped shaking, he suggested, "Why don't you go clean up? You look like you haven't had a bath in three days."

Caryl started to protest, then, realizing what he'd said, looked horrified. "Oh, I must look awful! Where is it?"

Carson pointed, and Caryl almost knocked down three people in her rush. He hoped they'd attribute her rudeness to a desperate need to get there in time. Caryl's appearance was one subject that engrossed her totally. She'd been known to change her clothes seventeen times in one day. She was *always* beautiful.

The next eastbound train on which they could get tickets left at seven in the evening. Carson counted what he'd have left—with enough out to eat. "How far north can we get on . . . thirty-two dollars, two children's tickets?" He didn't like lying about his age, but he really didn't look twelve and wouldn't take up any more space than an eleven-year-old.

The ticket agent consulted his book. "Rightway Station. That far enough?"

Carson nodded. Didn't sound like much of a place, but there'd be a phone. If he absolutely had to, he could always call Dad.

"OK," the agent said, took the money, passed over the tickets, and went on to the next person in line.

To Carson's relief, Caryl spent the remainder of the afternoon in the rest room. When he asked a woman to find out if she was still alive, he found that she had usurped the couch and was sound asleep. "She said she had to have some sleep," the woman told him, disgusted with both of them. "She had dark circles under her eyes."

Carson snorted, thanked his informant, snagged a newspaper and a couple of magazines out of the trash bin, and spent two hours alternately reading and trying to understand the news bulletins blared over the station's PA system. Something about gangs of looters and other criminals was an addition that bothered him greatly. The imminent arrival of the National Guard and their orders to shoot such people did nothing to make him feel better.

Caryl emerged at five-thirty with no dark circles. She was as well groomed as if she'd just left home on an ordinary day. "I'm hungry," she announced.

Carson got up. "C'mon. It's just a counter, so we'll have to stand in line behind a stool, but we should get something before they call the train."

Carson dreaded the scene Caryl would make when she discovered she'd have to wait. Fortunately, the newness of the experience interested her. Someone insisted that the pretty little girl should have a seat, so that crisis was averted.

Carson stood next to her, and they ate big bowls of chili. It was inexpensive and filling, and Caryl liked it. He had to shut her up when she wanted dessert. They didn't have enough money for that, but what Caryl wanted, she was accustomed to having. He wouldn't let go of her vocal cords until they were out of the lunchroom, and when she started to scream, he clamped down again.

"It's up to you," he said softly. "Keep your mouth shut, or I'll do it for you."

She fumed, but she shut up.

The trip east took four hours on a local, a special resurrected from the wrecking yard to drain off some of the flood of fleeing people. Carson wished he could tell those who had undamaged houses that the earth was stable now, and they didn't need to leave. The train didn't seem to have a schedule and sat at every station for such long periods that Carson felt he could have made better time by walking. They waited three more hours for a northbound train, listened, without wanting to hear, to more half-understood news about perverted people taking advantage of the quake conditions to enrich themselves, then had to crowd in with the last of the passengers and sit in an aisle on somebody else's suitcases. Shunted to sidings whenever an express came by, forced to wait while specials crawled past carrying heavy machines and tons of supplies to be used in the south, the train was over twelve hours late.

Carson sized up the situation early. At the second stop, he got off, found a twenty-four-hour convenience store, and stocked up on sandwiches and cans of juice. He had a feeling his money'd go farther this way—and they'd eat. He hid the big brown bag from Caryl and doled out food only every four hours—if she was awake.

Caryl sized up the situation, too, but differently. Even she could see that being a prima donna would earn her nothing but curses. She played the exhausted, darling little girl, and ended up sleeping across the laps of two motherly women. Carson discovered he could slide under the seats—this train, like the first, might have been built in 1830—put his head on his pack, and go to sleep, too. People were astonishingly kind about not stepping on him.

When the conductor pushed through the mob and told Carson the next stop was Rightway Station, Carson corralled his sister and collected their belongings. They sidled and excused themselves through the massed bodies until they reached the vestibule. It was crowded, too. *At least,* Carson thought, *we can't fall out.*

7

They jumped off the train onto a narrow platform beside a tiny station. Not one other person was in evidence anywhere. The single building stood in an endless stretch of desert, the only outpost of civilization in a land yet to be settled.

After the last twenty or so hours, the sense of isolation was both a relief and somehow threatening. Carson went to the ticket window. It was closed, and he could not hitch himself up and lean forward over the shelf far enough to press his face against the glass and verify his hunch that no one was inside. The hair on the back of his neck stood up straight—for absolutely no reason he could determine. The fact that there *was* a station, and that it was in a state of almost painful neatness and cleanliness, indicated the area was not deserted.

"It's only open on Fridays from eight to twelve o'clock," Caryl said.

Carson stopped trying to view the interior and went over to his sister. Taped to the windowpane of the entry door was a three-by-five card on which the information was neatly hand-printed.

"What day is it?" Caryl asked.

Carson's watch informed them of the time and the date, but the latter meant nothing.

"I don't know. Let's figure it out. The earthquake was Saturday." Of that, Carson was sure. The days since then blended together.

Caryl began one of her diatribes, but Carson, terribly aware of her, the only other living person for miles and miles, knew she was frightened and worried and showing it the only way she knew how. He ignored her completely.

"Sunday, we crossed the bridge," Carson muttered. "Monday was the smoggy day." He'd driven the Cat the next day. So Wednesday was the day he'd driven the jeep. This must be Thursday.

Caryl had run down. She stared at him. His total unawareness of her seemed beyond her capacity to believe.

"Thursday," he said. "We can make it until tomorrow at eight."

Caryl started in again, but ignoring her had been so successful that Carson continued it. He brushed her hands off his shirt and began an investigation of the premises. He looked through clean windows into a tiny waiting room. Nothing but twelve old-fashioned chairs and a wood stove—and an anachronistic modern pay phone he could use if he was willing to break in. He wasn't. Not yet. He thought the second door in the inner wall had a sign reading "Rest Room," and wondered where they'd . . . Plenty of deserted desert for that.

A narrow wooden walkway encircled the building, widening to form the station platform on the west and an entry porch along the east side. A graveled road from the southeast stopped at the front. To the south was a larger platform with a ramp leading up to it. Carson assumed it was used for the transfer of freight, for it was sturdily constructed, and the graveled area widened. Not so much as a tire track marred the even, raked surface.

Only two other evidences that life existed elsewhere broke the solitude and loneliness of the little station: the railroad lines and the row of telephone poles with their single wire.

Carson sat on the front steps. He was confused and a little scared. What kind of people built a station and a loading area, cleaned it, locked it, left it, and came back only once a week? He tried to decide. They were good builders. Carson's father would have approved of everything he saw. They did not litter, write graffiti, smoke, buy food or drink—or anything but tickets—at the station. They did not have electricity, gas, or running water, at least outside, and he assumed the toilet was self-contained. No solar installation, either.

What were he and Caryl going to do for the rest of today—and tonight—until the people arrived? What would *they* do when they found two children at the station?

Caryl, silent, sneaked up and sat down beside him.

"I'm thirsty," she said.

Trust Caryl to be aware of the present—and her immediate problems.

"You had a drink on the train before we got off—not

fifteen minutes ago. You just think you're thirsty because you can't find a drinking fountain. You can have a can of juice with supper. I filled your canteen, but it has to last you until tomorrow. Don't expect me to share mine. I won't."

She grabbed his canteen, but he had fixed it to his belt with this probability in mind.

"I said, 'No,' " he reminded her.

Caryl began her wail. At least she wasn't crying away her body moisture.

Carson stood and wandered up the road. It was hot—quite dreadfully hot—and it would get worse before it got better. Tonight was bound to be cold. They'd be glad they still had the sleeping bags.

The road curved. It continued across the arid land toward the hills. There must be a town beyond sight or concealed behind the first range. Maybe people lived in a valley over there, where they could drill for groundwater. Water every community had to have, even if it had nothing else most people would consider necessary.

He went back to the shady side of the building. Caryl had laid out a hand of solitaire and appeared to be completely involved in it. Carson knew she wasn't. She was just waiting for him to suggest rummy or another two-handed game, so she could turn him down. He sat back against the building and ignored her. He did not want to know what the radio might tell him, but his very unwillingness forced him to dig it out, turn it on low, and insert the earpiece. Death. Destruction. And the far more horrible reality of what some members of mankind were doing to others. He shut it off in despair and disgust.

While Caryl kept playing, Carson got up and walked into the scrubland for about a hundred yards. Not a single identifying landmark could indicate the spot at which he stopped—to anyone else. Carson knew he would be able to find it if he ever needed to. He wrapped in a plastic sack and buried most of his money, pocketing a dollar bill and three pennies of the four dollars and fifty-eight cents. Why, he wasn't quite sure, but if he ever needed that telephone, he wanted his useful change available. Caryl knew he still had some money left, or he'd have buried it all.

With sundown, the temperature plummeted. They had no fuel with which to make a fire, and Carson still could not force himself to break into the station. He insisted Caryl follow his lead—get into the down sleeping bags at once and try to go to sleep. She dragged her things around the corner, every movement and every word a comment on his utter incompetence. He listened—and sensed—to be sure she would not disobey his orders to leave the station alone.

She did not stay by herself for long. With the early moonrise, coyotes began their nightly hymns, and Caryl, terrified, rushed back to his side.

"Let me sleep with you, Carson. The bags are big enough. I'm so scared."

She was, and he almost agreed.

"Get your things," he ordered instead. "We'll sleep on your bag and in mine."

Arranging it took surprisingly little time. It was, after all, very cold.

Cuddled up together, they slept at last.

Day-old ham sandwiches were not Caryl's idea of breakfast, but she ate her share between complaints. Carson wished he'd been able to trust anything else to stay sufficiently edible. Ham made them both drink more than they should have.

They were very thirsty by the time the cloud of dust

along the road turned into three ancient trucks. They waited on the loading platform while the trucks pulled to a stop.

Quite a number of people climbed out of the cabs or off the tailboards. Regardless of sex or size, they dressed identically—sort of like Mexican peons: loose, long-sleeved shirts and equally loose, ankle-length pants, wide straw hats, thick-soled sandals. The fabric looked like unbleached muslin, much creased and sweat-stained, but extremely clean, considering the dust. Everyone wore his or her hair the same way—uncut, but pulled back and tied with a strip of material.

Carson stared. Caryl took one step and hid behind her brother.

She wasn't the only hider. Each of the smaller figures found a larger one behind which to shelter—and around which to peek. The people seemed as surprised to see Carson and Caryl as Carson and Caryl were to see them.

Did they speak English? Did they even speak?

Carson tried to swallow, had no saliva, and croaked out, "Hello. Do you have any water?"

That broke the silence. The people began acting like normal people, regardless of their appearance. Someone passed up a water bottle. They did speak—most of them at once—and although they seemed to have substituted the word "be" for almost every other form of the verb "to be," Carson had no trouble understanding. Plain speech, like that of the Society of Friends, Carson had heard before. This was not quite the same—although the people scattered a lot of "thees" and "thous" somewhat indiscriminately through their sentences, all of which were questions.

Caryl stopped hiding, instantly discerned which of the figures was the most motherly female, and threw herself off the platform into its arms. She hid her face, as always when she cried, so as not to display her tearlessness, and wailed.

Carson told about the earthquake, of which the people seemed aware—but with an attitude of semi-triumph Carson found completely unnerving. He explained that they were fleeing, implied they were trying to find their father. He explained they had come as far as his money would take them, expecting to find a small community where they could go to Travelers' Aide or Red Cross for help. He asked if the people would lend them money enough to get to the next town—trains came by every day and he could set up the signal. They seemed not to hear him. As he talked, a silent signal passed among the people. From the instant he told them about the earthquake, Carson had the eerie sensation that they heard nothing else he said.

"Come, thee," an older man said. "Thou'rt in our way. We must unload the trucks and and prepare to meet the train."

"I can help," Carson offered. "I'm strong."

"That do not be in doubt." The man smiled. "But thee has eaten nothing but unnatural food and has gone without water. Thee needs to rest."

Carson saw nothing unnatural in what they had eaten, and he did not feel in the least like resting. If he could have justified it in any way, he would have run into the desert. He had never felt this way—trapped by circumstance and strangers—and did not know how to deal with it. He let them lead him to a shady spot and seat him on one of the truck seats someone pulled out as if it were a familiar action. In a moment, Caryl was brought over to join him. She bubbled with gratitude and pleasure. He wondered if she'd lost her mind, but said nothing.

Carson watched as the trucks were unloaded. When the train pulled in, he tried to join the line of workers handing things into the boxcar. A woman, obviously concerned for his welfare, led him back to Caryl. Carson was about to tell Caryl they had to get on that train, even if they had to push people out of the way, jump aboard, and stow away. Another woman came over just then, sat with them, and gently combed Caryl's unkempt hair. She purred.

He considered jumping to his feet, screaming like a banshee, and trying to throw himself aboard. The muscular backs and arms of the men—and the boys—and the solidity of the line of bodies between him and his goal made him realize the futility of that course of action.

He stood up and started to go up the ramp. Perhaps he could at least call out. A definite gesture from the leader sent a boy somewhat older and larger than he to lead him back down. The grip of the hard, calloused hand on his arm was gentle, but Carson had not the least doubt that if he attempted to pull away, to turn and shout, to indicate in any way that he was not of their company, the hand would turn into a vise. Yet the boy only smiled in genuine comradeship. Carson wondered, quite suddenly, if he were the one who had gone crazy.

"Sit thee there," the boy said. "Thou'llt see. All will come right for thee."

It wouldn't, and Carson knew it, but he could do nothing to prevent the obvious intent of all these kind, hardworking people. He sat down.

As the train pulled out, Carson felt helpless, caught in an invisible purpose he could neither discern nor combat. Yet no one had offered him anything but kindness. He could not figure out why he felt so threatened.

How it came about that he was inserted into a truck cab

and taken with the strangers, Carson was not at all sure. Caryl was in the truck ahead of him. His mind, unable to direct his body, retreated almost into coma. His inability to determine his own actions recreated in him the sense of fear and isolation he had experienced upon alighting from the train. Even the fact that the people in his truck chattered cheerfully, tried to include him in their conversation—to be met with stolid, protective silence on Carson's part—and even began to sing, did not rouse him. Music had always calmed him, for he loved it, but this time, although melodious and harmonious, the singing affected him as would the screeching of the damned.

They paid his retreat no attention whatever. He might have been invisible, Carson feared. At last, some sense of self-preservation awoke, and he began to observe with preternatural acuity.

As he had guessed, the community was located on the opposite side of the range, the buildings set into the solid granite of the low mountains. The valley was extensively dry-farmed, with one section so green that he knew they were beginning to put in artesian wells and an irrigation system. He saw it all for the first time through a haze of dust and heat and unspecified worry.

The only buildings on the slopes were too large to be called houses. Near the top, set deeply into the side of the hill, was one small, separate building ("Our school," the driver pointed out proudly), then three long, narrow, wide-eaved bunkhouses. Lower down, a wide terrace held three buildings approximately twice the size of one of the bunkhouses and a flat space where the ground was being prepared for a fourth structure. Two outbuildings, too big to be just privies. Probably that and washhouses, as well. A little kids' playground with homemade equipment. A dirt playfield. A windmill and a water tank. That was all. Everything was unnaturally clean and neat.

The truck in which Carson rode and the one Caryl had jumped into both stopped before the first of the buildings. The third truck drove on to the one beyond.

The driver tooted the horn, and people spilled out of the buildings. Carson reacted as if the sound was acutely painful. He almost covered his ears, but his arms would not respond.

"Here be Jane," the woman to his left informed him. She pointed to a woman just emerging from the open door. "Come. She do be our greeter of new Followers."

What did that mean? Followers? At least his mind was beginning to awaken. Carson crawled out of the truck and stretched. Perhaps he could get back some freedom of movement.

In a moment, Caryl joined him, still burbling enthusiastically about how delightful these people were, how welcoming, how lucky they were to have been found by good strangers, not the awful ones they'd heard about. He wanted to slug her.

The trucks pulled away and were parked. The people began unloading and carrying supplies into the storehouse.

"I be Jane," the woman introduced herself.

Caryl supplied her name and Carson's, as he still remained silent.

"Come in. We'll get thee settled as soon as Pastor greets thee."

They waited in the relatively cool interior of the building—a large open space filled with trestle tables and benches, with other things upon which Carson found himself unable to concentrate.

Jane provided them with cool water and a hearty soup

that Carson's body demanded he eat although he thought he might throw up immediately. He did not. Caryl, picky, picky, poked about in the bowl trying to identify the contents. The smell was delicious, and she found herself too hungry to debate long. Down under Carson's semi-stasis, he grinned. Several vegetables in the soup were ones Caryl never ate. He watched her gobble, neatly, with her impeccable table manners. He wanted to slop and slobber but ate slowly and carefully instead.

"Ah, here be Pastor to welcome you," Jane said.

Carson looked up.

8

Carson's first sight of Pastor deepened the confusion from which he already suffered. Externally, Carson realized, the man was completely undistinguished. The leader dressed identically to all the others here, with the exception of a symbol Carson did not recognize that dangled from a cord around his neck—and he wore a black fabric belt wrapped around his waist. Yet the others all looked like peons, and Pastor might have been an emperor in disguise. *Napoleon, maybe?* Perhaps five feet six, slender, with slightly graying dark brown hair, unprepossessing facial features including a somewhat snub nose, full lips held with taut muscles so they indicated no softness, and small, gray eyes, Pastor could be overlooked so easily as to make him ignored in a crowd of five—if he stood still or did not speak.

The man moved with a purpose and energy like . . . like barely contained electricity. He seemed to take up twice the room of any man three times his size—and all of the oxygen in the air.

Entirely without intent, Carson rose to his feet. Caryl, obviously dumbfounded, scrambled to hers.

"Welcome to the Community of the Followers of the One Right Way," Pastor said.

Carson's internal debate continued. The man spoke as if conferring an imperial favor, yet the words struck pure ice through Carson's center. *The One Right Way?* he wondered. Many ways were right, for the people who held to them. So his father had taught him, and so Carson fervently believed. Was the man demented? How could he be, if all these people believed in him and followed his dictates? And they did; Carson knew it.

Having greeted them, Pastor showed concern only for their health and personal hygiene. Carson and Caryl were to bathe, clothe themselves appropriately for their new condition in life, and join the others at their work. Now that they were here, they would be expected to take their rightful share of the tasks at hand.

"But, sir," Carson began.

"Address me always as 'Pastor,' " the leader commanded. "I be no noble, to have a worthless title."

"Pastor," Carson conceded. "Please, may I speak?"

Where that request came from, Carson was not sure, but it did stop the man's turn away.

"Speak."

"My sister and I don't want to be here. We came because your people wouldn't let us get on the train. We're trying to get north, where we can get in touch with our father."

Pastor smiled. Carson felt as though he'd scream. "The Followers knew you had been sent to us," the man said. "Now you do not know what you want. You will soon learn."

The sense of trying to penetrate an impermeable wall with which Pastor surrounded himself was so clear that Carson simply stared. Nothing he could say would have the least effect! He might as well explain mechanics to the wind.

Defeated, at least for now, Carson allowed himself to be led off to the men's washhouse. He bathed and dressed in the clothing set out for him. He had become a Follower, whatever that was, at least outwardly.

He sat waiting on the bench outside the washhouse for over half an hour, listening to Caryl's change in attitude. She apparently threw a real tantrum, although she did not attempt to make magic. *She must be* really *scared,* Carson thought.

"I *won't* wear those awful clothes. They're scratchy. I won't go around looking like everybody else—a million years out of date. Where are my own things? You've stolen them! You're thieves! No, I won't let you tie my hair back like that. It'll pull out all the curl." Not a question was given an answer, no raised voice responded. Only affectionate address and gentle, reasonable insistence met her fury and nastiness.

The boy who had led him down the ramp showed up before Caryl had emerged.

"Welcome, Carson," he said. "I be Joe. Come. I'll show thee around."

"I'm waiting for my sister," Carson responded. "She's really scared and worried."

"My mother will care for her," Joe said. "Thee can do nothing to help her, only make her less willing to accept. That will not make it easier."

Carson stared at him. True, it would not make Caryl's adjustment easier. But, as he didn't want her to adjust to this life, he was ready to grow roots into that seat.

Joe shook his head. "Come. I do wish to be thy friend."

He meant it. Carson always knew. How could he fight this? He sighed and stood up. "OK," he said. Later, he'd get together with Caryl some way.

He didn't. He hardly saw her.

During the next week, slowly, almost as if he and Caryl were not to be told, but come to realize the truth themselves, Carson learned enough about Rightway Community to understand why he had so strongly resisted the idea of coming here. It was a commune. Not like the communes he had read about in Modern American History, in many of which drugs, indiscriminate sex, and a generally lax attitude toward conventional mores had been practiced, nor exactly like the communities of the early Shakers, Amish, or Mennonites, either. *This* was the home of those who believed in The One Right Way—a Way shown to their leader, Pastor, by God Himself. Armageddon was coming, as signaled by the earthquakes for which they had waited nearly twenty years. The heathens would be eliminated, the earth cleansed by fire, and they, in their God-chosen protected valley, would remain to re-people the earth and spread the doctrine of The One Right Way. Carson and Caryl had not ended up at Rightway Station by happenstance. They had been sent. God intended that they become members of the Community of Followers. How could they possibly doubt it?

This one terrifying idea and the fact that he and Caryl

were never permitted to be alone together negated, for Carson, all the positive attributes of life here. The people were truly committed to a peaceful way of life. They treated one another—and Carson and Caryl—with a loving consideration that was rarely broken. Everyone worked, even the little ones of about four, who did such tasks as setting and clearing the tables for the communal meals, feeding chickens and gathering eggs, and collecting every burnable scrap for the fires. In keeping with the "render unto Caesar" doctrine, Rightway Community had a school, modern textbooks, and an excellent, dedicated teacher. Every child attended until the age of sixteen. Rightway Community produced good products, all from the farm or made by hand, and sold them for fair prices; it kept books, paid every cent of its taxes, and obeyed the laws of the land with exactitude.

Not only hard work and good diet made the Followers' bodies so hard and muscular. Each evening after they had rested following the meal, the floor was cleared, great mats were rolled out, and every person from the age of four participated in karate. Carson, who had always wanted to learn one of the martial arts, asked if he might join in. No, but he and Caryl might watch. They were not ready to attempt so strenuous an activity—would not be for several weeks, until their bodies had been refined and purified by life On The Way. Carson nearly bit his tongue to keep from responding angrily.

Caryl's behavior mitigated into silent resistance within three days. Being a darling, beautiful, stylish little girl who looked so frail a good breeze would blow her away disappeared into being an undistinguishable member of the group of children. Carson watched, one noon, as a woman removed the bows Caryl had tied onto the braids she had plaited into her hair.

"Don't do that," Caryl screamed. She jumped up so hard that the table shook and food spilled. "You leave my hair alone. It's mine! I like it to look pretty. Not all hot and sticky down the back of my neck. If you want to look and feel awful, that's your thing. It's not mine! It never will be. Leave me alone!"

All the time she yelled, she was scrambling out from between the girls on either side. They tried to stop her, but she swiped at eyes and wriggled like an eel and managed to free herself from the bench and table. She grabbed the strips of cloth and turned to run away.

The woman took a couple of long strides, encircled Caryl's waist with one arm, and picked her up, horizontal, kicking and screaming. No one could possibly have heard the woman's words, but Carson got the impression that she was speaking both gently and lovingly.

She bore Caryl over to a door, opened it, and deposited her burden inside. Caryl rushed forward but was pushed back. The woman closed and locked the door.

Carson attempted to get up to help her, but Joe, who seemed to be his shadow, put a hand on his arm. "It do be all right," he said softly. "It's well ventilated. There's a pallet to sit or lie on. And water. When she can act according to The Way, she'll be let out. You can't help her by preventing it."

Carson felt so helpless that he hated himself. His stomach knotted so hard that he wondered if he'd developed a bleeding ulcer. But at least nothing inside Caryl's cell could be thrown or otherwise moved. She was too smart to do without water. She certainly wouldn't be happy, but she wasn't in any danger.

He was unable to finish his meal.

What would happen if Caryl demonstrated her magic, Carson did not know, but he feared it. The rigidity of this life, the absolute adherence to a code the Followers accepted without question, kept him always aware of Caryl, always ready to prevent her from using her mind-power. She was not working hard enough yet to expend her extra energies in physical labor. Her internal power was building to an explosion, and Carson did not know whether he could control it.

If he couldn't, what would happen to them? Should he let Caryl put on the demonstration of power she well could in the hope that Pastor—Carson was never to learn his worldly name—would have them taken back to the station and allowed to go somewhere else because they were not fit to be Followers of The One Right Way?

When he had his second interview with Pastor, Carson discovered that permitting Caryl to mind-move would be extremely dangerous. Worse, he feared it would lead to difficulties far greater than the ones they had. He tried again to explain they wished to leave, but was curtly informed he was here to listen and to learn. The only words he might utter were "Yes, Pastor."

Pastor believed Carson and Caryl had been sent here by God. "The Followers are being tested to prove our fitness to be God's chosen instruments. How can we spread The Word to survivors if we cannot correct one ill-mannered child, one raised Off The Way by parents who permitted her to develop as she has? She is but an instrument in God's plan, a representative of all we must face. No, boy, we must—and we will—win your sister to The Way."

Carson had heard of people so consumed by a single idea that nothing else could enter their lives, but he had never before met one. The reality of this man's devotion to his cause was terrifying. He tried not to shake.

"If you love your sister—and deluded in your methods

74

as you are, I believe you do—you must help her. God has told me that we must persevere until seven times seven times. Should anyone given such opportunity refuse to accept The Way, He will take such recalcitrants to His bosom."

Pastor's enraptured face, the eyes gleaming with a fervor of religious passion, turned away.

Carson could not believe, but did. *Take them to His bosom?* Directly? How? By killing them?

The expression Pastor turned on him was so sorrowful that Carson nearly believed himself incorrect.

"We shall have been proved yet unworthy. More trials and dedication, greater allegiance to The One Right Way shall be demanded. Oh, what penance will be required of us!"

Pastor's sorrow was for himself and his followers! Not for the person!

Carson's fear was so great that it triggered a long-repressed reaction. As he could not fight and he could not flee, his anger woke, consuming him as entirely as Pastor's *idee fixe* did the man. Rage, controlled and keen, pushed the helplessness and terror to the side. Carson listened, aware, making certain that nothing he could learn would be missed. He would find a way, *not* Pastor's *One* Right Way, to escape! Regardless of what Pastor threatened, he *would*. He might take months to figure out how, but he would. Nothing, not even the Followers, could prevent it. He would do whatever he had to do bar murder: lie, cheat, steal, dissimulate, pretend. His fury rose. They were forcing him into the kind of life he most deplored.

His personal considerations did not prevent him from hearing—and recording permanently—what Pastor said. He feared he might never forget it, that he would live with the sentence of death—his and Caryl's—always at the back of his mind.

"God, in His infinite wisdom, will require that such persons be cast out into His desert, to live or die at His will. If they do, indeed, lose this life, it will be to come into His presence to be cleansed and reborn, free of their worldly egos."

Carson was terrified and infuriated when he realized what this meant—the Followers believed themselves instruments of grace and *justified* in murdering anyone who would not accept their Way. He went cold and shaking and broke out in icy sweat. He managed not to vomit until after Pastor dismissed him.

9

The almost ungovernable passion of his first fury passed, leaving Carson oddly weak but no longer detached from the life around him. He set upon a plan to convince his captors that he was accepting The Way with more and more alacrity and commitment, for only so would he obtain freedom of movement and the opportunities to learn what he must know. Much of the time he hated himself for his hypocrisy. Occasionally he earned rewards so surprising and unexpected as to make him pause and wonder.

Caryl was the only baby or small child with whom Carson had ever dealt; consequently he did not like either. This attitude dissolved first. All the little ones here were so loved, so secure, so generally happy and good that he found himself doing exactly as everyone else did. A great deal of carrying about, hugging, helping, and enjoying the children was the rule. When N'omi, who could barely walk, toddled over to him, laughing and trying to give him her simple plaything, Carson broke into chuckles himself.

"Hi, N'omi," he heard himself say. "Good girl. C'mon, want to upsy-daisy?"

He picked her up and swung her high. She chortled and gooed. *Fun,* he thought. *She's never known anything but fun and love.*

The idea sobered him. How could he manage to put this universal goodness together with being kidnapped and imprisoned—and with what would happen to both himself and his sister if Caryl didn't begin to come around?

He lowered N'omi and held her against his chest. She examined his sober face, patted his cheek, and made baby sounds that indicated a question.

"It's OK, N'omi," he said. "Want down now?"

She did, and he held her carefully until she got her balance. The baby's mother, Ahura, grinned at Carson as she held out her arms for N'omi to toddle to.

"She really loves you," the woman said. "I be glad. . . ."

"Glad I love her back," Carson said. He knew that wasn't what Ahura meant, but it would cover the otherwise awkward gaffe. What she meant was "I'm glad you're learning to Follow The Way." He wasn't, but some things about it were good, like babies who were loved and wanted, who didn't terrify their mothers.

When the fourth Friday arrived and neither Carson nor Caryl was among the crew to go to the railroad, Carson did not dare ask directly if he might go. He hoped he had convinced the Followers that he was accepting The Way, but making that request might solidify any suspicions. That

Friday his determination and stubbornness awoke free of the anger that had proved an enemy of both thought and action. He knew enough now that he should start seriously to plot escape.

He did not like to take advantage of their differences, but the Followers had left him no choice.

Followers of The Way did not eavesdrop or violate the privacy of any other person's thoughts. So little privacy of person was permitted to anyone that privacy of the mind was absolute. He could overhear much no one realized he listened to. He became a constant eavesdropper—and learned little.

How and when could he get free of them? At night? Well, possibly. He slept in the bachelors' house with a dozen others, all boys from the age of twelve in one room and all unmarried men of whatever age in the other. The doors had no locks, and only unthinking conformity kept the youngsters inside after they had been sent to bed. He would hold that possibility for later. It was too easy to be caught.

Married couples slept in tiny cells in the middle barracks. When they had children, another room was allotted next to theirs, where their children slept until they entered puberty. Even Pastor took for himself and his wife no more than the two rooms. When the church was completed, he would have an office wherein he would instruct his charges individually. For now, instructions were given in his sleeping cubicle during the midday break for meditation.

So each afternoon during the hottest part of the day, Carson lay on the rooftop of the middle building, shaded by the hilltop, to meditate. Though the others knew where he went, no one suggested he not go there. Everyone chose a private place to be alone. The fact that he lay near one of the ventilation holes leading to Pastor's quarters was not obvious, and no one in the community would make the connection—they simply did not think that way.

He overheard much he promptly forgot, not enjoying his position or his activity. References to himself or Caryl justified his eavesdropping. Followers sought Pastor's advice on how to deal with their anger and distress at Caryl's behavior. People wanted to like Carson, but they felt he "did not be" completely open with them. How could they help him to trust, to believe? A Friday team-leader suggested they show him their trust—take him with them to the train. Pastor vetoed it. Not until Carson had been here for a year, had memorized the entire *Book of The Way*, and had made his commitment to The One Right Way as an adult could he be so tempted.

He could not live in this gentle prison for a year! He *could not* believe as they did—that God was their own private property, and only they had His ear and His word. He didn't believe in their Armageddon—despite the earthquake, which was *not* caused by the hand of God reaching down and shaking His world—and he never would!

Carson saw little of Caryl except at a distance, although he was never unaware of her. The crews were established monthly. Carson and Caryl had been put on two different ones when they arrived, and when the new crew lists were made up, they were still not together. Pastor separated them intentionally, Carson knew, so they could make no plans together. Also, if each had no one to share memories with, both would forget more quickly. That, too, Carson overheard. It infuriated him. His daily meditations were conscious remembrances of everything about the real world—everything except his slavery to Caryl. That he still suffered under, though no one knew but he.

Caryl worked more. Carson sometimes saw her with other children in her crew, anonymous in their cream-colored clothing and straw hats. When she had her own row to weed, he let her do it with her mind. She used her telekinesis to help carry loads, stir pots, scrub wash—ways where it was almost invisible—and not noted because others were not aware it occurred. Caryl was exhausted by the heat, the change in diet, the hard physical labor, and most, by the need always to keep her temper. She was forced to turn some of her psychic energies toward mastering the act of living. The Followers made Caryl act as if she were unimportant, insignificant. She was saving up. One day, they'd find out how important Caryl was—when she paid them back! Carson was always wary. She'd adapt to the physical living conditions—Caryl was a most capable child—and when she did, he'd better be ready.

What was he going to do? Daily, Carson became more desperate—and more determined.

The site of Rightway Community had been chosen deliberately, far from any other settlement, reachable only by their one twisting road, fully twenty-five miles from their railroad station. No water, no shade, nothing to live on between Rightway and the station—and no water even there. But there was a phone, and Carson could learn to work the signals at the station to stop a train. The only plan he could make required use of a truck, and Pastor's orders were all too obvious. Carson was not permitted in the parking area without a friend. Neither was he allowed to enter the building in which the other machinery was stored.

School classes were held from six-thirty in the morning until about nine in the evening, except for meal and game times, in order to free different groups of children for their tasks. One morning Carson pelted downslope with his crew. They were to weed corn today, hours in the hot sun, making sure no other roots took up the little moisture. This corn was like nothing he had ever seen. The teacher had explained that they grew a special kind of Indian maize, one adapted for dry conditions. Usually, the boys piled into a wagon behind a tractor and were driven down to the field. Today everyone stood around the tractor in a concerned group. No one had attention left for him, so Carson made his way to the front. Something was wrong with the tractor, something nobody seemed to know how to fix.

"A chance!" Carson almost announced aloud. He knew all about engines, all about every kind of moving vehicle he could get the manuals for. Tractors were nothing new.

The driver was going over what was wrong—and what he'd tried to do—for what must have been the sixth time. Carson listened intently. No wonder things kept breaking down! The Followers in charge of the machinery seemed to know less about it than he did.

Silence descended.

"Have you cleared the entire fuel line?" Carson asked. "Do you always filter the fuel? The injectors could be clogged. Where's the manual?"

The quality of the silence changed from one kind of worry to another. "For the sake of The Way!" he burst out. "Do you want it fixed or don't you? If you don't, I'm going to go hoe corn—which anybody else can do better. 'Take advantage of the skills and talents of all and each. Set each Follower to those tasks for which he is best suited.' Wasn't that in last week's Lessons?"

He pushed his way through the group, grabbed his hoe, and started down the path. For his entire two-hour shift, behind his half-shut eyes, he reviewed the diesel and tractor manuals, grateful for the kind of mind that remembered what it saw—and could reread what it had read.

The next morning Absalom, who drove the tractor, met him at the schoolroom door. "Pastor says to see if what thee knows can help me fix the tractor," the man said.

"OK," Carson agreed.

He was not allowed to touch, only to look and to draw diagrams or write out instructions. They determined, as he had half suspected, that the tractor suffered from old age and inadequate upkeep, and several parts had to be replaced. The storage building proved to have the ones they needed. Not new, but properly rebuilt, the parts had been bought at the same time as the old machines—for exactly this purpose.

For the first time, Carson felt relatively at home and comfortable in Rightway. He itched to get his hands dirty, but accepted the situation as well as he could and made one good suggestion after the other. When Absalom and his helpers were done, the tractor shone with cleanliness and oil and new paint. The men knew much more about its upkeep, and Carson believed it would run for years— if they kept up the maintenance. The mechanic drove the rejuvenated machine out of the parking area to the shouts and cheers of all.

Followers were generous with honest praise. "It do be all Carson's work," Absalom declared. "He do know all about machines. We were just the hands."

"Great hands," Carson said, not wanting to draw more attention to himself than he already had. "I've only read about it, never done it. I couldn't have repaired it by myself."

"Thus it is proved that God sent you here," Pastor pronounced. "The Followers need your skills."

Damn! Carson thought. *Just what I don't need. One more reason to be here. Damn, damn, damn.*

From then on, he was assigned to any crew whose work included a machine. He didn't get to use it, just to watch and to make suggestions. Several of his ideas resulted in the saving of both time and labor—and, in one case, prevented their drill from being set up in such a way that it would destroy itself. He should have been happy, but Caryl, furious at her former slave's growing importance and independence, came closer and closer to tearing herself apart. Her condition never let Carson forget his primary purpose.

One by one, he answered his list of questions. How much fuel did it take to get to the railroad? Where was the fuel kept? How did one funnel it into the tanks safely? Who had the keys, or where were they kept? What peculiarities did each vehicle have? What were the differences between driving one of those and driving a more modern vehicle? He would have no opportunity or time to experiment, as he had had with the Cat.

Desert living, hard work, constant anger, worry, subterfuge, and seemingly futile planning kept Carson always tired. The Followers wondered at his slow adaptation to The Right Way, but put it down to being raised Off The Way. They did make it the excuse for continuing to exclude him and Caryl from karate instruction. Carson understood—and seethed. Followers practiced absolute nonviolence—up to the point where they or The Way might be threatened. Any eight-year-old could have taken Carson down and kept him there.

Day after boring, endless day passed, each so like the others that Carson could hardly keep track of them. Pastor had taken his watch, as well as his money and the radio and everything else he and Caryl had brought with them. Partly, this was in payment for what they received in return, and not an unfair bargain. They were, after all, housed, fed, educated, and protected—overly protected—and although they certainly worked for their keep, so did every other individual in Rightway. Partly, Carson knew, their things had been confiscated because they were reminders of a life lived Off The Way. To keep his chronological bearings, Carson counted Fridays—Train Days.

Everyone else counted Sundays, Lord's Days, and Carson didn't blame them. Lord's Day was mostly fun. Short service, good meals, games, old-fashioned dancing, and lots of singing to the music of guitars and a fiddle and the big overstrung upright piano in the Common House. The hour of religious instruction, in the late afternoon while adults prepared the meal, was bearable only because it meant no work. Despite themselves, Carson and Caryl memorized chapter after chapter of *The Book of The Way.*

They had objections, in Caryl's case violent objections, to the topics of instruction Pastor chose for that fall: the responsibilities of children toward adults—absolute obedience based on absolute conviction that the adults Followed The Way—and the responsibility of adults toward children—to bring them up On The Way without deviation. The only time a child was physically chastised in this society was if he or she failed to accept, like the necessity for oxygen, every word of *The Book of The Way.* After Caryl screamed out that the righteous teachings about men owning women was nonsense and Pastor caned her on her bare legs so hard that she bore bruises for a week, she kept her opinions to herself.

That hour on Sunday was the most difficult of the entire

week for Carson, and he dreaded it. He had to try to memorize, to appear to pay attention, and to answer correctly when called upon, yet to control Caryl the entire time.

Caryl had never accepted other people's opinions of how she should believe and behave. All her anger and frustration here concentrated upon Pastor. She hated him fiercely, totally. Uncontrolled, she might well have found a way to kill him. She would have felt as totally justified as the Followers would if they decided she and Carson must be cast out—to die.

10

The tenth Sunday, the pattern broke. A visitor arrived—the first non-Follower Carson had seen since his arrival. He was an old man, the kind his father might have described without disparagement as a "desert rat." He hiked in at dawn, following his mule.

Carson discovered himself unable to get close to the visitor, carefully screened from his attention, sent on unnecessary errands, put to work out of his crew duties on the few things that had to be done. He was furious but concealed his feelings. Caryl tried to get the man's attention, but someone put a hand over her mouth, picked her up, and took her to that little room, where she stayed the entire day. The old man did not appear to notice. How could he? He was surrounded by loving people, all of whom were delighted that he had come to visit. Yes, they would keep his ore for him in the safe; yes, they had sent his order off with theirs several weeks ago, the cans and packages of food were here. He must have a wash and a good breakfast and join in the celebrations of Lord's Day.

The only good thing about that Sunday was that Caryl, locked away, was not present at instruction, so Carson was relatively free. He ached with frustration and helplessness. The first time he might be able to send a message had arrived, and he was forestalled and prevented. He did very poorly—so poorly that Pastor sent him to the bachelors' house with a copy of the Chapter for today, and told him he would be fed, but he might not come out until he had memorized it.

Alone, Carson cried as hard as he knew Caryl cried alone in her prison. What could he do? These people were so good, yet they treated him and Caryl as if they were the worst kind of criminals by denying them contact with the world outside their jails. He could not square the genuine love and care he felt around him, experienced daily, with this one terrible injustice.

He refused to memorize. Let them leave him here forever. The boy who brought his evening meal set it inside the door. Without a glance in Carson's direction, he closed the door and left.

Carson did not feel hungry, but he ate every scrap of the food. The possibility he'd tucked away for later snapped into his mind. Wait for an hour or so, then go scouting. The possibility that he would disobey Pastor's order would never occur to any of the others. Almost, it had not occurred to him! He would try for a truck. If that didn't work, he'd find a way to write a note and put it in the old man's gear. If he got caught, he wasn't sure what they'd do to him. They might cane him or make him go without food or both. He'd better be prepared.

When the community was entirely dark except for the lights in the Common House, Carson blew out his lantern and left the room. Laughter, music, and sounds of general rejoicing poured out of the open windows. He avoided the lighted squares and went quickly to the parking area. Since Carson had been working with the machine crews, Pastor himself kept all the keys, including those to the shed where they stored the gasoline and diesel fuel.

Can I hot-wire a truck? Carson wondered. *Well, check the fuel tanks first.*

Too little fuel in any of them, and nothing with which he could siphon fuel from one to another—if he wasn't caught in the act. He could not drive near enough to the railroad. They'd catch him before he'd hiked the rest of the way. Unless he put the other trucks out of commission? He couldn't. Little as they knew about them, the Followers depended upon those trucks, and they'd never be able to repair any damage without Carson's knowledge and assistance. *Besides,* he thought, *might as well set off a siren as try to open one of those hoods.*

Well, that left the other possibility. Carson moved through the darkness to the schoolroom with the ease of a blind man in his customary habitat. The school, too, had no lock. Why should it? No one here would steal anything.

Carson found a pencil and a sheet of paper. He needed enough light to write legibly, so he scrunched himself against the wall of the Common House under a window. On the unlikely possibility that anyone looked out the window, they wouldn't see him. Somebody might come out to use a washhouse, but they'd be blinded by the sudden change from light to dark. He took a last look around.

Two lights sped nearer along the road!

Carson's astonishment kept him still long enough to prevent his leaping to his feet, shouting in triumph. The burst of hope switched into cold fear at what he had almost done—given away his first real possibility of escape. He sat still, breathing through his mouth, calming himself so he could think. He must be very careful. Too often had he experienced the Followers' control.

The road ended here, and there was nothing between the station and the commune, so Rightway was the only place those vehicles could be coming. The cars were still a long way away—so far that he could not make out the double beam of headlights, only two moving points of light. They could not be here in less than twenty minutes; thirty was a better estimate.

Were Pastor and the Followers expecting other visitors? He did not believe something so unusual could have been kept from him—unless none of the boys knew, which was possible but not likely. But perhaps. He began to write his note.

"My name is Carson Bleeker," he wrote. "My sister Caryl and I tried to get away after the earthquake. We ended up at Rightway Station, and these people brought us here. They will not let us leave. Please, please help us get away. Our father is Daffyd Bleeker. Call him collect at his office, (043) 221-7791. *Please* call him and tell him where we are."

Writing the note gave him another idea. Two possibilities were always better than one. He copied the words on the bottom half of the page and folded the paper back and forth several times, running his nails down the fold each time. The two halves pulled apart silently. If he could get to one of the cars, he'd slip the note in. Then, even if the Followers prevented his talking with the visitors, he would have that extra chance.

Carson tucked the pencil under the edge of the building and sneaked to the barn where the mule-packs had been stowed.

He'd forgotten the mule! It might bray and give him away. Carson knew nothing about mules, but he hoped they were enough like other animals that this one would be asleep.

The mule was asleep, or seemed so. Carson shoved one of his notes into the pack-sack of food, ready for the old man when he left. He knew a little more than he had. Old Ed was a prospector, a man a hundred years out of his time, who chipped a living from long-abandoned mines. He didn't make much, but enough for a grubstake and the little cash he needed to continue living the way he wanted to. Rightway had semi-adopted him, as he seemed willing to accept The Way as long as they did not expect him to stay. How he was able to come and go as he chose was something of a mystery to Carson. Surely the Followers could keep him here as easily as they did a couple of healthy children. Maybe not. Old Ed had transportation, and he obviously knew how to get along in this country.

Carson stole to the barn door and listened. Nothing yet. Where should he go? He was sure visitors would be invited into the Common House. His first inclination was to rush up to the cars before the Followers could stop him, but he had to consider the possibility that the arrivals were expected. He wanted to find out who they were, be ready to . . . not rush in a door, for the Followers would stop him . . . to leap through a window and beg for rescue, if there seemed any chance he might be helped.

The parking area lay between the storehouse and the barn. He'd stay where he was until the cars arrived. When the visitors went inside, he'd put the note in a car and ghost over to a window. Even if they left someone on watch—

and why on earth would they?—he could go out the back door and creep up to listen where no one could see him.

Deprived of his wristwatch, Carson had learned to estimate time by his breathing. In about ten minutes the vehicles drove up and stopped outside the Common House. The visitors were strangers. They hadn't known where to park. *Thinking like a Follower again!* Carson could have kicked himself. He ran around the back of the storehouse and peeked out to watch.

People spilled out of the Common House. First Old Ed, now another set of visitors—in the same day? Such unusualness.

Carson could not make out words, just a generally confused noise. Four men in the first vehicle, a vaguely official-looking station wagon, got out and were greeted. The four men in the second, a jeep, remained with it. The visitors were invited to come in.

Good! He could go over to the jeep as soon as everyone was inside. Should he? Somehow, the fact that all the men didn't enter seemed odd. He started twice, stopped, and decided to find out more first.

He wouldn't need the note. If things went his way, he could talk to the men. If not, he didn't want it on him should he be caught. He tore it into tiny scraps and blew them off his palm. He waited another few minutes. Then, hoping the men in the jeep weren't watching this area, he ducked low and ran over to sit under a window again.

He listened intently. Pastor's voice, accustomed to being heard, cut through and hushed the general conversation.

"Let the sheriff speak," he said.

Carson almost leaped through the window. A sheriff! A chance to get away! He did stand, hands on the sill, to look in as if the open window were a two-way mirror. The attention of everyone inside was on the four strangers.

Something about those men was wrong. Carson could not pinpoint the source of his conviction, but the sensation was so strong that he could not move. He remained, stone-still, watching and listening.

"We're from the county seat," the middle-sized man with the star on his shirt said. "I'm Sheriff Barnwell and these are my deputies, Selkirk, O'Halloran, and Welles."

People murmured.

What was it? Why couldn't Carson move? Why did he know that whoever these men were, they were not a sheriff and his deputies?

"We've come to warn you. All kinds of people have left the earthquake areas. Most of them are just honest folks, hungry and tired and in need of a place to stay. A few are undesirables—the kind who could make a lot of trouble for people like you, who don't believe in fighting."

Carson sank down, gripped by the same cold fear he had experienced when he'd heard the radio reports of people who looted and killed after the earthquake. He peeked in again, this time carefully.

The exchanged glances and comments indicated that the Followers were concerned. To Carson, the Followers' re-action registered fake, but that might have been because he knew how deadly dangerous these people—men, women, and children—could be if necessary. The murmur rose again, only to still as the sheriff continued to speak.

"One gang is particularly dangerous. They've been traced to our county. If we're right, they're likely to be heading here. Think like one of them. Your community is little-known, hidden, has no lawmen, and no communication except by one road that'd be easy to booby-trap. You have food and water and supplies and . . ." The man paused, and Carson could see his pretense of concern. ". . . I don't like to say this, but you've got to be warned. Women."

The horror within the room was almost palpable. The man had touched a nerve. If there had been doubt, it was gone.

The man went on, "You're rumored not to use banks and to have a lot of money here. Those things will draw criminals: a secure, hidden place to hole up, women, and money. I felt you'd better be warned. I've deputized a group of honest men, and I'll leave four of them here to protect you."

The buzz in the room rose. Carson could make out few sentences. The speaker seemed to have worried them. But the idea of non-Followers?

The man had made a mistake. A real sheriff would know Rightway Community would accept no one who didn't Follow The Way, even for protection. Wouldn't a real sheriff know about the self-defense training? Were these the things that made Carson so sure the seemingly straight-forward man was a ringer?

The man moved a little, and the star on his shirt caught the light. Carson nearly gasped. Six-pointed star! Not seven! Sheriffs wore seven-pointed stars. How could the man be so stupid? Did Pastor know?

Carson watched Pastor, evaluating every expression, every slight movement. He had made a study of this man, learning much he felt sure Pastor did not know he revealed. Could he read whether or not Pastor was only pretending to accept the sheriff and his deputies?

"Er, ah, Sheriff," one of the deputies said, "what about strangers, people they don't know?"

Carson knew it was part of the act—the scenario these men had planned before they came. They wanted to know if there had been visitors, people who'd come and gone, taking information with them, or people who were still here, people who would fight.

He pulled his head back, away from the opening. Why, he wasn't quite sure, as no one seemed to be looking around, much less out the windows. He crouched below the windowsill, listening with every pore.

"I'm a vis'ter," a voice said. Old Ed, the prospector.

"We know this man," Pastor interjected. "We have known him for years. He is a Searcher for The Way."

"You've been back in the hills?" The sheriff's voice, to Carson, took on a new note, one of faint menace . . . or a question other than the one he'd asked.

"Not s' far back I ain't heerd about them low-lifes from th' city yer talkin' about," Old Ed said. "I tol' m' frens about 'em afore you got here."

"Ah. Then you'll agree your friends need protection, I'm sure," the sheriff said.

"It's a reason I come."

"Anybody else?"

"Only two young children, a brother and sister sent to us by God to become Followers of The Way," Pastor assured him.

"Ah, Sheriff, remember th' last place?"

That man was responding to cues, saying things Carson knew he'd been told to say if any outsiders—even two young children—were here.

"I don't like to say this . . ." the leader began. Carson knew he did like to say it, that he'd planned exactly what to say, in case. "There've been rumors that the gang has a couple—maybe more—kids they use as decoys. Send them in ahead, get information, then move in after them. I think it'd be a good idea if I talked to these kids. Make sure they aren't the ones we've heard about."

Carson broke out in cold sweat. The man was . . . hopefully triumphant? Cold, cruel, determined, he'd found what he *really* searched for! Them! Him and Caryl.

Why?

Dad might have offered a reward!

Why should the man radiate menace, if all he wanted was money? He did radiate menace, an aura so thick that Carson could hardly breathe.

One of the women had been spooked. "Shall I get the boy, Pastor?"

"No. He be studying *The Book of The Way*. When he learns the lesson, he will join us."

"He could've gone to sleep. It do be a long time, and it be getting late."

"Then the Lord has decreed his sleep, that he may waken rested and in the proper frame of mind," Pastor said. "None shall disturb him."

"How about the girl? She be right here. She—well, she seems . . ."

Carson knew how Caryl seemed. The Followers would rather believe Caryl was a decoy than that she was truly led here. Any child so resistant to their teachings must be one of those who must perish. These men would take her away. The Followers would not have to continue to put up with her. What an ideal solution! They had not failed—they had been tested.

"Bring her out," Pastor decided. "You may question her."

Lord God Almighty, Carson prayed, *help me!* This was Caryl's chance! Here was her opportunity to pay him back for every unacceptable breach of discipline. What could he do?

He sat so frozen with both fear and worry, desperately trying to make plans to counter whatever Caryl might say, might do, that the slight sound behind him went ignored. A stabbing pain in his shoulder alerted him, but too late. He sank into almost instant blackness.

In that instant, he realized that the men from the jeep must have been watching and listening, too. Probably they had gone to the bachelors' house to get him, had found him absent, and had begun searching. They'd come prepared. He could make no outcry, no indication that he was . . .

11

Carson was aware long before he could move, even to open his eyes. He could not feel his body and almost succumbed to overwhelming panic. Nothing else horrible happened, and he began to hope that since he had his mind again, he would soon have his body back. He breathed deeply, counting breaths. In two minutes, he felt his tongue. He kept it very still. Otherwise he could bite it so deeply that he'd bleed to death. No. Someone had put padding between his teeth and tied it firmly. An effective gag, true, but probably a most humane method of preventing him from harming himself. That indicated Followers, not his attackers, but he still did not know where he was. He hoped the bindings were not too tight.

As he conquered his fear he accepted his immobility.

At least no one would know he was awake. He could listen, try to find out what had happened.

Voices Carson recognized verified that he had not yet been removed from the Community. He pieced the scenario together from various sentences he overheard. *He was being taken away. Caryl had to stay. Her pleas went unnoticed.* Something about him made these men determined to have him and the Followers equally determined to cast him out. He concentrated all his attention on hearing everything he could.

A man whispered, "We got our witch!" Someone kicked him to shut him up.

Witch! Carson thought. *Caryl! They know she can mind-move! Who? Road crew? Only ones who've seen her do it. Long way away. Doesn't matter.* These men knew. They'd been searching for her. Caryl found out, and in terror of what happened to witches, she'd made them all believe *Carson* was the mind-mover.

He'd pinpointed his source of menace!

Carson had white nights occasionally, when every method of getting to sleep only made him more wide awake. One such night years ago, on his way to the kitchen . . .

"Caryl's a telekinetic, Elisha." Dad's voice.

"What does that mean?" Mother's. And not too slurred.

"A person who can—and does—move physical objects solely by using the power of the mind."

"Giving it a name doesn't make it any easier to live with!"

"Granted. But we *must* keep her hidden. Think of the thousands of children who are stolen every year and never located. Caryl's abilities make her potentially valuable to thieves and even more violent criminals. Think what they could make her do."

Carson hadn't been really hungry to begin with, only in

99

search of a legitimate reason to get out of bed. Dad's words had sent him back upstairs as silently as he'd come down.

Criminals had *him* in their power, believing *he* could mind-move!

What would they do to him when they found out he couldn't? Kill him? Terrified, Carson couldn't even shudder. He didn't want to die! *Stop it!* he commanded himself. *You're not dead yet! Think of something else!*

Caryl. Think about Caryl. That'd make him mad enough to stop being scared.

It didn't. He knew the men would come back here and get her. It would serve her right, but it meant he'd be dead.

The dull babble of voices became louder, and a door opened. Carson listened to save his life.

He identified voices: Pastor, the fake sheriff, and to his surprise, Old Ed. Pastor bade the sheriff good-bye. The door closed.

"Whatcha mean, y' think y' otta test th' boy some way? Th' girl sounds nuts t' me," Old Ed said.

"That's the point, Ed." The leader's voice held such false camaraderie that Carson wondered why Ed didn't gag. "I think she could be wrong, too. We could make a bad mistake—thinking this kid is the telekinetic we've heard about. If he's not, and he probably isn't, then we should either bring him back here, or if he wants to go back where he came from, see that he gets there. If he is the one, we know we have to handle him very carefully—probably keep him doped until we can get him to the authorities who're looking for him."

Logical, Carson thought, *but lies. Ed, don't believe them!*

"How y' plannin' t' test 'im?"

"You're familiar with this area. Isn't there a place we

could put him—say, in an abandoned mine—in the dark, tied up, and see if he could cut himself loose and get out? That'd prove the girl was right. If he doesn't come out by a certain time we'll go in and get him. Then we'll bring him down here and leave him or take him along to town."

Smart, Carson thought. *Have Ed show them a place they can use for a temporary hideout until they can find something better. When they find out I'm not telekinetic, they'll . . .* He refused to finish that sentence. It ended in his death.

"Yeah, there is a ol' mine, back a ways inta th' hills. I checked it out, in case th' miners'd left any ore. Gets dangerous, iffen y' go too far in. Part of it's safe enough. Y' kin put 'im in there an' see if he kin get out by hisself. That otta do it. Kin y' figger any kid'd sit in th' dark iffen he could witch up a flashlight 'n' get out?"

The old man couldn't possibly know he offered Carson a hope! The boy was no less terrified, but he clung to the wisp of possibility.

What'll they do to Ed after he shows them? he wondered. *Kill him? Stop it! Just listen!*

"How far is it?"

"Hour, hour 'n' a half's walk."

"Is there a road? Can we take him there in the jeep?"

"Not from here. There's a ol' mine road, but it comes in from th' other side. Only a mule track from here. I got a good sturdy mule. I'll haul 'im in fer ya. Only cost y' fifty bucks."

Why didn't Carson feel menace from this voice? It was properly whining and avaricious.

"Water in the mine?" The man's voice sounded casual, but Carson knew the answer was essential.

The old prospector spat. "Stream back in some. Stinks, an' tastes like th' inside of a cow barn, but it don't make y' sick. I've drunk it of'n enough. OK, if y' hold yer nose."

The men apparently left the immediate area to confer. Carson could not make out words. When they came back, they agreed. The sheriff and three others would go with Ed to take Carson into the hills. The rest would wait for them to return.

Carson realized he had made an intuitive leap and had not known it. From the moment he'd come to, he'd thought of *these* men as the gang the fake sheriff had described earlier. Carson was now ascribing all their speeches, actions, and reasons to that assumption. Their willingness to hike through the desert night along what the old man said was an unused mule track fit the pattern perfectly. Obviously, Pastor had convinced them that Rightway Community was not without defense—a highly dangerous one. They needed somewhere else to hide out. The old mine might serve until they could find something better.

"How long's th' kid gonna be like this?" Old Ed asked as the men manhandled Carson over the mule's back.

"Doc?" the leader asked.

"He'll start coming to in a couple of hours," a voice Carson hadn't heard before answered. "I was set up for an older, bigger kid. No harm, but he'll be out for long enough."

"Get the other flashlights, Spider," the leader ordered. "Let's get going."

"Nothin' t' burn up there," Old Ed warned. "Iffen yer gonna sit around an' wait, y'd better pack in some wood."

They borrowed some from the commune's woodpile and tried to put it on the mule. Old Ed stopped them. The kid was all the load Stubborn'd take. Carson wondered at that. Why *am I not scared of Ed? Is he on my side?* If the four men carried the wood themselves, they'd be more tired when they got there.

Carson remembered little of the trip. His body was coming back to him slowly, and it hurt. He tried to concentrate on the route with his inner senses, but they weren't working. He kept his eyes shut with second-by-second determination. With his luck, somebody'd be shining a flashlight at his face if he slitted his eyelids one millimeter for half a second.

At last the rocking, climbing trip came to an end. The men left him hanging across the mule while they built and lit a fire. The desert nights were cold, and Carson had lost sensation in his feet and hands again. He hoped they weren't frostbitten.

"Leave him tied," the leader said. "If he's the one we . . . we've been told to look out for, he'll be able to cut himself loose."

Carson's heart sank.

"An' iffen he ain't?"

"We'll wait until he's had plenty of time, then we'll go in and get him. He'll be OK that long."

The man lied. Carson knew it.

He was awake body and mind now. Should he let them know? If he could only get a hand free, or even his mouth, he could . . .

A hard, calloused hand swatted his backside. It seemed to say, "Keep still, boy." Carson felt . . . protected? . . . warned? He remembered the wood and stayed quiet.

They proceeded through the mine tunnels, Old Ed leading the mule at a steady pace. In a place Carson usually could have mapped with the accuracy of a CAT scan, he was pulled off the mule and dumped on the floor. He groaned a little.

"Y' leave 'im like that, he'll be so stiff an' cramped up he won't be able t' crawl, much less walk out," Old Ed said. "Here, I'll straighten 'im out some."

As he was rearranged, Carson felt steel at his wrists. He

managed to keep his pose of drugged relaxation only because he was terribly aware of every second, every sensation. His wrists were free! He was so relieved and grateful that he almost blacked out.

"That'll do, old man," the leader said.

"What y' in such a all-fired hurry fer?" Old Ed said. He stood up. "Y' got a hour or so t' wait."

"Let's get out of here!" Another voice made it clear that one man would not welcome hiding out in a mine.

The sound of a hand-slap on a furred rump. "Out y' go, Stubborn. C'mon, mule, back up a ways."

The footsteps and voices retreated, taking the light with them.

"Hold it." The leader must have turned back toward where they'd left Carson. "You sure there's no other way out of here?"

Old Ed's chuckle bounced off the rocky walls. "Sure there's a way. Takes about three hours, goes clear through th' mountain. Lotsa gangways off it. Like one a' them mazes in th' paper. See that dark hole? That's where y'd start. Any a' you think y'd duck inta there iffen y' could jest walk out th' easy way?"

"Hell, no," another voice said. "I'm goin'."

When he could no longer hear the barest echo, Carson sat up and freed himself from his bonds. His emotions had taken greater trauma than his body, and he was internally numb. He felt intense thirst. The smelly little stream was only thirty or forty yards back along the tunnel. When he had worked some blood back into his hands and feet, he rose, flexed, and slowly made his way to it. Taking Ed's advice, he held his nose and drank deeply. He did not breathe until he was back in his side-tunnel, and the air held less stench. Yes, bottom of a birdcage. Yuck!

Carson sat in the darkness and thought. It was, after all, the only thing he had to do until the drug no longer suppressed his extra sense.

If the old prospector was telling the truth—and why would he lie? It'd have been easier just to tell the gang the mine had no other exit—Carson could duck into that hole, take the long way through the mountain to the other exit, and free himself. He need not go back to the men— or to Rightway. Causing a rockfall to block off this way, so the men would believe him dead, would be simple. And then what? Like it or not, Caryl was his responsibility. Would the men suspect that she was the one they wanted?

He'd figured out that the sheriff and his men were ringers; Caryl would, too. What would she do then? Well, worrying about her wouldn't help her any.

Pastor, realizing exactly what the men were, had seen his opportunity to get rid of Carson, who was thirteen now. No longer a child, he was not becoming a Follower. Followers celebrated no other birthdays, but at thirteen each child starred in a most important ceremony—rather like bar mitzvah—that officially declared him an adult. No ceremony had been held for Carson.

The words of *The Book of The Way* on the subject of children flicked into his mind. If someone behaved as Caryl could, it signaled the coming of Armageddon, when the Devil would insinuate himself into people, making them do ungodly things—like telekinesis and telepathy and teleportation, no doubt. So long as the person was a *child,* Pastor knew ways to make the power of the Devil do the work of God. When the child had done God's work thoroughly enough, unrelentingly enough, and long enough, the Devil would retreat, leaving the child free of his curse. The child was not to blame, but must work to become free. No, Pastor would not send Caryl into the desert, and even if the men returned for her, he would *not* let them take her. She was his Sacred Responsibility.

Caryl had learned to control herself pretty well, but once she got over being scared, she'd get angry. She'd build up to an explosion. Then they'd know who the witch was. Whatever Pastor decided to do to free her of the "Devil's curse," Carson knew his sister would hate it.

Carson wished he didn't know Caryl so well. She'd feel completely justified, thinking she'd done only what she had to do. She *had to* keep people from thinking she was a witch. Here was her chance to pay him back for every time he'd kept her from doing something she wanted to do. Here was her chance to be free of him.

He almost shouted as the next thought flashed into his mind. If he stopped controlling Caryl, she would believe him to be dead. She'd find out what it was like to be free of control when one lacked self-control. Pastor would see to it that Caryl took the consequences of her behavior.

It had all worked out for the best. He was free, or would be soon, and near enough to the commune that he could get back, steal a truck, and get away. Now he had the time to think, he knew how to solve the problems. Hot-wiring was done under the dash, so he needn't open the hood. Get the big shears from the tool-board in the unlocked barn. Cut off a length of the hose used to fill the animal's trough from the water tank. Use it for a siphon. Fill one truck's tank from the other two. Let all the air out of all the tires on both trucks. He'd think of other things that weren't either permanent or beyond their ability to repair. The Followers knew him too well to believe that he'd do more than delay them as long as he could. He'd go to the nearest town, not the station, get a real sheriff or other law official, and come back for Caryl. For once, she'd be glad to see him!

He hoped she lived until then.

That thought surprised him a little. Did he really? Or was it just his memory replaying the broken record of Mother's sentence? He began, for the first time in his life, to examine his beliefs, his feelings and their sources, the reasons *why* he thought and believed and acted and reacted as he did.

For example, the men had been so sure that putting him alone in the dark, dangerous, abandoned mine would terrify him into running into their arms. But he had no fear of darkness whatever. The mine was perfectly safe, for him, because he knew exactly what not to do. From Carson's point of view, the men couldn't have chosen a better place for him.

He smiled into the darkness. Kind of like Brer Rabbit. "Throw me into the river. Throw me into the fire. Only please, please, don't throw me into the briar patch!"

A remembrance, very vague and far away, edged into the rim of his mind. He didn't try to force it, but leaned back against a solid spot, looking at black and wondering.

12

"I'm sure glad you're with me." His father's voice spoke in Carson's memory. He let the rest of the recall roll over him.

"Why, Daddy?" five-year-old Carson asked.

"Let's see if I can explain," the other voice answered. "You aren't scared, are you?"

"No. Should I be?"

A small chuckle. "Of course not, but almost everybody is—in darkness this complete."

"Why, Daddy?"

"Most people get scared when they can't see. They're so used to seeing that when they can't, they don't know where they are. They bump into things, and trip down stairs, and hurt themselves. Often, they can't get out of the darkness even when there's a way. That's bad enough, but it leads to worse. For some reason nobody quite understands, being completely surrounded by darkness makes many people start to imagine that the things they're afraid of are in the dark, waiting to hurt them. Like having a bad dream come true."

Before Carson could think about that, his father continued, "You're not scared in the dark. You don't need to see because you sense where things are. Since you know, you don't hurt yourself—and nothing imaginary can frighten you."

"Do you know about things in the dark, Daddy?"

"Where everything is, the way you do? No. I wish I did. But I think I know something just as good, in this case. I know every inch of this building—as if I had a map in my mind. You know where everything is by sensing it. I can tell you where to go and what we want to find, you can find it, and we'll be out in time to get home before Mother starts worrying that something serious has happened to us."

"Like a car accident?"

"That's right. We don't want Mother to worry, so we'd better start."

"OK, Daddy." Carson didn't want his mother to worry. She'd be alone with Caryl, whom she was afraid of—though Carson didn't understand that very well.

"Let's see. We were standing in the door to the computer room when the lights went out. I haven't moved, but I don't know if I've turned away from the door. Have I?"

"Um-hm, you're looking toward me."

"Take my hand, please, son. Now. Lead me down the hallway to the right—past the place where the trash is stacked—to the narrow door in the left wall. Can do?"

"Sure." Carson took his father's hand, and they set out.

Carson remembered how simple it was. The only thing that bothered him was all those stairs. His legs got so tired. They were four stories below ground in the building to which his father had taken him to show his son what he did for a living. The huge complex was the first on which Mr. Bleeker was chief project engineer, and he was proud of it. When the electricity went off—Mr. Bleeker assumed a blackout in the city, not some problem confined to the building—the elevators no longer worked, so they had to climb the steep, narrow access stairs. His father would have carried Carson, but his balance was not sure in the darkness. He feared a stumble, a fall, and greater harm than simple exhaustion.

They'd moved slowly but accurately. The access doors were locked, but Mr. Bleeker had the keys, and Carson could put them into the locks. They counted landings. At the fourth, they let themselves out into a corridor on the ground floor. Carson heard his father's quiet sigh of relief as they came around a corner into the lobby, where the less dark of the moonlit night poured in.

While Mr. Bleeker locked the door behind them, Carson ran as directed to the telephones. One was installed for use by people in wheelchairs, so Carson had no trouble reaching it to call Mother and relieve her mind. She had been frightened—but mostly for them. Caryl had been asleep since four. Mother had candles and flashlights. She was all right because she could see. Carson remembered being sorry for Mother, who had to see in order not to be afraid.

Only now did he realize that his father was equally to be pitied. More, for he had had no candles, no flashlights, and a small child he must not frighten with his own fear.

Carson discovered himself thinking very gratefully about his father, appreciating the courage that journey in the dark at the end of a small hand must have taken.

Mother accepted the fact that he had certain unusual abilities only after Caryl came, and they discovered that Carson could keep the baby from doing things that terrified Mother. Daddy had always understood and accepted his talents. Daddy was the one who'd taught him never to display them.

"People who don't have certain abilities either envy the people who do—envy is a kind of hate, Carson," he'd said, "or they pretend the ability either isn't there or isn't important. Few people can be trusted with secrets like your talents."

"So I shouldn't show or tell anybody? I should keep it our secret?"

"Not forever, son," Daddy said. "But until you're a lot older. OK?"

"OK, Daddy," Carson agreed.

Carson had kept the secret, and so had his father.

13

Carson stretched. A faint glow accompanied the movement of his left arm. A what? He bent the arm and looked closely at his wrist. The sense of constriction around the wrist was not the result of the long period of binding. He was wearing his wristwatch.

He examined his clothing. All of it, including the warm jacket that kept out the cold as his Rightway clothing would never have done, was that he'd worn when he got off the train. He felt around for his pack. *For Pete's sake,* he thought. All this time he could have been sitting on his sleeping bag. Well, his dopiness had a logical explanation.

How thorough of Pastor. Nothing of Carson remained in the commune. To check his assumption, Carson checked his pockets. In addition to things he expected—his wallet, the matches, and the folded-up wad of tissues—he had money. He presumed it to be a dollar and three cents. The size and feel of currency were unmistakable, and pennies were the only coins this size.

He checked the time. In a half hour or so, the effects of the drug should have worn off completely, and he'd be able to use his extra sense with confidence. Ed had seen to it that he had much information. Did the old man realize that?

Carson thought a lot about Old Ed, too, in a very short time. The conclusions to which he came could only be proved right or wrong by what happened during the next few hours.

As the drug lost its hold on him, he found himself thinking much more clearly and objectively. His first intention had been to search for the old miner's other way out as soon as he could, but he realized he could not simply leave. He must return to within earshot of the end of the main tunnel. Almost everything he knew was the result of intuition and reasoning, not information. If he could overhear more conversation, he might discover whether he was correct.

If the men weren't there, he'd steal down to the community. Tonight, when no one was expecting him, would be his best opportunity to commandeer a truck.

As he had neither food nor water he was willing to drink, he'd have to steal supplies, too. If he could figure out a way to get Caryl, he decided, he would take her with him now. Only if he could not rescue her without being captured himself would he leave her.

He decided to take his pack and set it inside the entry to the second exit. Its size and weight surprised him. *Did they put all Caryl's things in, too?* he thought. *Is this why they couldn't pile the wood on the mule? The pack and I together were too heavy?* He shook that idea off immediately.

For that matter, why had the pack been left with him? He dug into it to see if anything could give him a clue. Yes, all Caryl's things seemed to be here, too.

At the bottom was a flashlight. He pressed the button, and the resultant flash nearly blinded him. He sat back on his heels and tried to understand exactly what the flashlight meant.

What he'd heard made him doubt that the kidnappers knew much about telekinesis. They seemed to believe that a mind-mover could simply grab objects from one place and have them appear in another. Caryl couldn't. She had to see what she moved, or at least know what and where it was. And what she moved remained in normal space; nothing disappeared from one place and reappeared somewhere else.

But the kidnappers did not know that. They had gagged him and tied his hands so tightly that they'd have been permanently damaged if Old Ed hadn't cut the ropes. Or if Carson couldn't untie the ropes with his mind, as the kidnappers apparently thought he could if he was the telekinetic they were looking for. *They'd believe I could get at the flashlight if I was a witch,* Carson realized, *but not otherwise. And I'd need the flashlight to find my way out.*

He found something he could not explain—two full canteens. Surely the men wouldn't have allowed that if they'd known, and Pastor wouldn't have permitted him to have water. He must have a friend in the community or . . . Old Ed, though how Ed could have managed it, Carson didn't know.

He shoved the flashlight and canteens into the pack,

closed it, slung it over one shoulder, and started for the adit. His confusion and his fear of the callous, conscienceless men hung in the air like smoke. He did not want to take the chance that they might discover him, but Old Ed was out there, too. If Ed had indeed helped him, the old man might need *his* help.

Carson felt danger before he came to it. He made his way through the place where a deadfall had been constructed. Its presence shocked him. *I must have slept,* he realized. Not that sleeping would have been unlikely—with all the stuff Doc'd pumped into him—but his feeling of trust in the old miner dwindled. If Ed were out there, why had he gone along with this? Or had he? Was he still all right? Now Carson had a second reason for going to the entrance.

Regardless of what the facts proved to be, he had one surety: the deadfall. If it had no other purpose, it proved that the kidnappers believed he could get out of the mine safely only if he had a light.

He wondered if the sheriff and his gang had enough curiosity—and credulity—to wait and see if he could make his way out. He supposed they would. Telekinetics were few, and even if they couldn't operate as the men seemed to think they could, a telekinetic in the power of criminals could make stealing and looting a lot less dangerous—for the criminals. He must be extremely careful. He knew exactly what they'd do if they'd kidnapped him because he could mind-move, then believed he was lying when he said he couldn't. So far as Carson knew, what he could do, his own abilities, didn't even have a name.

The firelight beyond the mine entrance signaled the presence of the men. Carson crept, staying on the darker side of the corridor where the turn cast thick shadows.

Not a pebble moved. No grit of rock-shard beneath his feet gave him away.

He heard voices. He took four more steps, stopped in the deepest shadow, and listened.

"Well, he ought to be coming to about now," said Doc.

"How much time do we give him?"

"One hour. If he's not out by then, we trip the deadfall and wait until morning," said the leader.

"An' if he comes out? He's gonna see the fire."

"Can't be here for another half hour, anyway. The stuff I gave him turns off psi functions."

"We'll put it out in twenty minutes or so, take our positions, and watch for a light in the mine," the leader said.

"Gets cold, hereabouts, in the dark."

"Gets a lot colder in hell, I hear."

"What's that s'posta mean?"

"Knock it off. Mack, stop heckling Spider. All he means, Spi, is that if the boy is a witch, like the girl said, he'll come out, trap or no trap. If he comes out, he's not going to like us much. Might even throw a few well-aimed rocks, if he has a lighted target. By splitting up, we're pretty safe. The others can get to the kid even if he locates one of us with the flashlight. If he doesn't come out, we find another place to hide out. Then we go back and get the girl. But we wait and find out."

"Oh. OK, Boss."

"You sure conned that old geezer. He was real sure we was the law. All that deputizing him so he'd tell us if there was a place we could bring the kid. Thought I'd jump when he said it was only a hour away—an' there was a road we could use t' get the cars up from th' other side."

"Yeah, and gittin' 'im t' pack the kid in on the mule. I was sure we was gonna hafta carry him."

116

"An' how you got him t' go back t' the commies so we could set the deadfall. Ol' man like him shouldn't be out all night in th' cold. T'morra, he can show the other deputies how to get up here on that old road he talked about t' pick us up. Another trip fer him, fifty bucks when he comes back."

"I don't get that, Boss. Why'd y' want 'im t' come back?"

"Who's going to be our witness that we did nothing to the boy—if he doesn't come out, that is? If he does, Doc'll drug him again, and the old guy'll take off inta the hills. Or so the commies'll think."

"Smart, Boss."

Carson shuddered. Yes, these men were planning to kill—him if he wasn't their witch, and Ed if he was.

"So we wait till the old guy's shown the others the route up here in the cars. Then, if the kid's the one we want, we see that the old guy has an unfortunate accident and we've got outselves a hideout. If the kid doesn't come out, what's-his-name—Ed?—Ed goes into the mine because none of us will. We heard this big noise; we know there's been a cave-in. He's the expert. He goes in and discovers the rockfall with the kid under it. We had nothing to do with it. It's all the old man's fault—we took his word the place was safe. Poor kid. We leave when Ed does. Too bad we'll be cut off from the stream by the deadfall, but that stinking water's no loss. We'll find somewhere better to hole up."

"We gonna hit the commune, Boss?"

"Not worth it. You were outside when he told about their physical education. Karate for everybody over four, every night. That pastor's a black belt, and he's not the only one—even a couple of the women. Only way to handle that kind is to shoot the whole lot—and we'd have to bury them if we stayed there. And what would happen Friday, when they didn't show up at the station? The law's none too bright, but it's not going to ignore that."

"What about th' safe?"

"Mack, tell them."

Mack grunted. "Y' know what they keep in there? Books! Like Bibles. A lotta good they'd do us. I even left the cash box. All forty-two dollars and change."

Yes, Carson thought. The conversation proved his hunch that Pastor knew who these men really were. The Community must have had several thousand dollars—as well as Old Ed's ore—in that safe. Pastor had sent someone to clear and restock it before Mack checked it. The Followers did not believe in violence, but neither did they believe in permitting the violent to harm them. Dissimulation and enlightened self-interest could make violence unnecessary, if one were neither simpleminded nor too trusting. Pastor was neither.

Setting aside unanswerable questions regarding the kidnappers' beliefs about telekinesis, Carson realized that all of his assumptions had proved to be true. The men were exactly what he had thought they were. But Old Ed, by cutting him free, had saved both their lives.

Carson decided to set off the deadfall. Those men would never believe he could have escaped, so they wouldn't look for him. As soon as they left, he could get out and away.

In the morning, the old man would bring the others up. They'd make Ed go into the mine, where he'd find a huge fall of rocks. He'd presume Carson's body to be buried beneath it, and so report. They'd let him go down to the Community to carry the news, and they'd take off in their cars.

Rightway Community would hold a ceremony: Carson's funeral. The Followers would believe he died because he had refused to Follow The One Right Way, thus was dead in soul anyway. Pastor would know the truth. His belief that Carson must die on earth in order for his soul to be cleansed in heaven would sustain him and prevent him from feeling guilty.

The funeral offered the best time for him to return to the Community if he had to do it in daylight. But then he'd have no chance of getting Caryl away. He'd have to go alone.

How would Caryl feel when she attended the funeral?

If she were left alone, he doubted that she'd be too upset. After all, she had nothing whatever to do with actually killing him

Unfortunately for her, Pastor wouldn't leave her alone to work out her justifications. He'd instruct her in guilt, all right. Every member of the Community would shun her. Lack of guilt and repentance would prove she was a doomed, damned child of the Devil. She had lied to protect herself and thereby had killed her own brother.

Oh, how she'd hate him then!

Carson retreated into the mine silently. He had the information he needed. Now, to see if there was indeed another exit . . . if Old Ed had told the truth. At least he felt no ill effects from the water he'd swilled down. He drank from the foul-smelling stream again to save his fresh water and to keep clearing the drug out of his system. His extra sense felt acute. He could soon discover whether the gallery in which he stood was the only exit, or if there was another, three hours away through the mountain, that he could approach through the natural-appearing hole. He ducked into it and leaned against the rock, sensing with his entire body. A long distance away was another exit from the mine. Old Ed had told the truth.

An idea struck him. If he tripped the deadfall, the

kidnappers would think that he was the witch but hadn't been careful enough. Believing that might prevent them from kidnapping Caryl. He went back and examined the deadfall. Somebody sure knew how to make and set one! Just a touch there, the lightest pull on that string, and that piece of the old mine-prop would move. Carson almost grinned when he thought of the men lugging all those pounds and pounds of rocks to pile just so.

Now, how could he trigger it without being caught? *Hm. Yes. That rock, then* . . . No. Better simply to throw a large rock against the string and run like hell.

The deadfall dropped with a reverberant roar and crumble. Any number of large boulders catapulted after him down the gallery, but none of them hit him. Carson leaned against a wall to get his breath and to examine the new conformation of the rock-pile. If he had to, he could get out this way, but he wanted to be sure they couldn't come in after him.

Carson walked, climbed, crawled, and clambered, never at a loss for direction. By continuing both in and up, he would come through the spur at a higher elevation. He found a narrow side-tunnel and moved quickly along it. At one point, he sensed that the tunnel had turned, but it had been filled with rock from a newer cut that led straighter. That seam had probably been worked out, and the miner—he felt sure it was Old Ed—had found another streak here.

Shortly after two o'clock, Carson sat several feet back from the end of the tunnel. He rested. He was hungry, tired, and at a low ebb in his sensory keenness. He leaned back against the rock wall to store up some strength.

Dawnlight woke him. Blast! He'd wanted to be at least halfway back to Rightway by this time. Then he could have rested, to make the remainder of the trip during the long dinner and karate periods when few people were outside, none looking for him. He would need food soon, and he knew the Followers' schedule well enough that he could steal supplies with little difficulty. He also knew a couple of places to hide until they were all busy with his Farewell Ceremony.

He was so hungry, and his mouth felt like old leather. The drug had left him thirsty, and he had drunk all the water in one canteen. He must save the other for the long trip over the mountains to Rightway. The only other water he knew of was miles back through the darkness, and it smelled so awful that he'd almost rather go without. Well, he'd go into daylight for a while, anyway.

He crawled to the opening and sensed out. A man's body sat there.

"Carson," Old Ed's voice said, "I know yer in there. C'mon out. I got grub fer ya."

Carson crawled out. He sat up and looked at the man.

A thick sandwich wrapped in a bread-wrapper lay on the ground with a tin cup of water beside it.

"Go ahead, eat," Ed directed. "Then you 'n' me're gonna hava talk."

Carson drained the cup first, then wolfed down the hearty cheese and canned-corned-beef sandwich. Ed refilled the cup.

When he'd finished eating, Carson waited.

Ed nodded. "Now, I wanna hear what y' got t' tell me."

Carson couldn't find words. He'd tried, all the time he was eating. Ed waited.

At last, Carson decided the old man deserved a lot more than he could give. After all, Ed had saved his life.

"I'm not telekinetic. I'm not a witch. I'm not part of any

gang. I didn't have anything to do with stealing or killing. That's the truth."

"I know that," Ed said, "but y' got outa th' mine."

The silence, this time, lasted at least two minutes. Ed waited.

"I promised my dad," Carson got out at last, "that I wouldn't talk about that."

Ed's nod was large and slow. He made a considering sound.

"Figures. OK. S'pozin' I tell y' a story. That way, you ain't doin' th' talkin'."

Carson nodded. He owed the man more than he could pay. He could listen.

14

"Once upon a time," Ed began, his eyes twinkling in his bearded face, "there was this kid. He come from a fam'ly a' smiths 'n' miners. When things got real bad in th' mines, an' a chance come t' git t' America, his gran'folks pulled up stakes and headed out."

It's not my story, Carson thought in surprise. *It's his!*

"Now this fam'ly, it always done good. Good work, good pay, good grub, good women. Somma th' lads went t' th' forge, but most went inta th' mines, and th' girls married miners. There was, some said, good luck hangin' aroun' these folks. Not alla th' boys had th' luck, but th' fam'ly stuck t'gether. One lucky one to a crew. None goes down iffen th' lucky one don't. That was th' way it was in th' ol' country, 'n' fer quite a spella years, that was th' way it was here.

"But the young folks begun marryin' outa th' bunch that'd come over t'gether. Come one day when th' luck run out, an' this fam'ly wasn't special no more. But by then things was different in th' mines. There was unions, an' OSHA, an' new machines, an' fresh air, an' all kindsa things, so nobody missed th' luck much.

"But t' git back t' th' kid I started with. After he'd got beat good, too many times, fer tellin' lies about things he couldn'ta no way knowed nothin' about, he shut his mouth. But when he got t' be six, somethin' special happent.

"His ma drest 'im up in his Sund'y best an' slicked his hair down good an' took 'im on th' bus. They got off by a big brick buildin' with grass an' trees aroun'. It was sum-mer—when th' kid's birthday was—an' when they got offa th' bus they walkt across th' grass to a bench under a tree. There was a ol' man sittin' there. Real ol' with watery eyes an' a cane.

"Th' kid, he was some scairt. Th' ol' man was *so* ol', an' he drest funny. Th' kid didn't wanna go, but his ma had aholda his wrist, and she'da dragged 'im, so he went.

" 'Now, then, Da,' his ma said to th' ol' man. She pulled th' kid aroun' where th' ol' man could git a good look at 'im.

" 'Now, then, our Mary,' th' ol' man said in his wheezy ol' voice.

" 'This here's our Ed. He turned six on Thursd'y.'

"The ol' man nodded.

" 'Say hello t' yer great-great-grampa,' th' ma said.

"Th' kid was more scairta his ma's heavy han' than he was a' th' ol' man, so he said, nice an' loud, 'Hello, Great-great-grampa.'

124

"Th' ol' man laft. 'Gramps'll do,' he said. He picked up his cane and whapped it onta the bench beside 'im. 'Sit here, our Ed. You 'n' me're gonna hava talk.'

"Th' ma pusht th' kid a little. When th' kid'd climbed up 'n' sat, danglin' his legs 'n' not knowin' what t' do with his han's, his ma lookt down at 'im.

" 'You speak up, an' you speak true. I'll be back in a hour. We hafta take th' three-ten bus.' She turned and walkt away like she was mad.

"Th' ol' man didn't look at th' boy. He just began t'talk. He talked about the fam'ly, and th' mines, and the luck, and how he was the last one who had it, and how he kept hoping, hoping and waiting, for one more, just one more of the lucky ones."

The hair on the back of Carson's neck rose. Something was happening to Ed's speech.

"The boy couldn't say a word. He just sat and listened to the old man tell of the knowing: knowing about the rock, and the safe places, and where it was not safe, and about not needing light to show you where you were, because you knew, and feeling everything around you—where the streaks lay, and how the seams turned, and everything. Not feeling with the hands, but knowing with the luck.

"Then the old man turned and looked straight at the boy. 'Are you the one I have been hoping and waiting for?' he asked.

"Now, th' kid knew he was, 'cause what he'd got beat fer was just the kinda thing th' ol' man talkt about. He couldn't tell th' ol' man—he'd been tol' t' speak up an' speak true—and true was what Ma said it was. An' th' ol' man had his big cane.

"But there was something about the old man, something

the lad could feel in almost the same way that he knew how far away the wall to his right was, and where the next rain would bring down part of it. He knew how much the old man wanted him to be the lucky one.

"He finally figured something he could say, something he could tell his ma—because she'd ask him."

Ed's voice, his accent, even the timbre and pitch, belonged to two different people. Carson stared in intense, half-frightened anticipation.

" 'My ma tol' me never t' tell no more stories fer true,' th' kid began.

" 'What kind of stories?'

"The old man and the lad looked at one another. The child didn't mind the watery eyes, or the old smell, or even the cane anymore. He just held his breath.

"The old man said, 'You and I have a long wait. As long as you're telling *stories,* and we both know that's all they are, you're doing just what your mother told you. And you're making an old man happy.'

"The lad noticed it seemed harder for the old man to talk. Maybe, if he talked for a while, Gramps could just listen.

" 'Well,' the boy said, 'Once upon a time there was this kid. . . .' He told his great-great-grandfather about what he could feel and know and sense—but always as if he were telling a tale.

"His gramps breathed hard, and his face got strange-looking, but the old man took a little bottle out of his sweater pocket. He shook out a little pill and put it under his tongue. In a minute or two, he looked some better.

"When the lad finished his stories, his grandfather leaned over toward him and said, very softly, 'Now, if this were not all just a story, as we both know it must be, I would tell you that you are the one I have waited for. I would say to you—if you were the lucky one, that is—that you have a Gift, a Gift from God, to tell you about the earth and the mines and the dark places in each. A Gift to use to help all the unlucky ones who do not have it. If you were he, I could say these things to you.' "

Carson could not breathe. It took a conscious act of will to get his lungs working again. Ed was no longer the old western prospector, a hundred years behind the time. He had become an even older man, a man with a high, clear, old voice—a voice with a totally different inflection. The drawl and the western accent had disappeared completely, replaced by a sound, a lilt, a pronunciation Carson could pinpoint like a dart homing on center. Even now, his father's family had it—the Welsh sound. He stared transfixed with unbelief.

" 'I would tell you that the Gift is a silent one. To speak of it, to tell those who do not have it, brings swift retribution. I would tell you to cherish it and use it in silence, for your good and for the good of others.' "

The beautiful Welsh tenor made the speech almost a song. It died away, and Carson wanted it to come back so he could listen and listen.

When Ed spoke again, the old prospector had returned.

"Well, th' boy's ma come awalkin' along th' path then, and th' gramps reached inta his pocket, quick-like. He pulled somethin' out and pusht it inta th' boy's han'. The kid caught on quick and dug inta his pocket fer his hanky. He left the somethin' in his pocket. He handed th' hanky to his gramps, who took it an' wiped th' runny places on his face.

" 'This is a good lad you have here, Mary,' th' ol' man said t' th' boy's ma. 'We have had a good talk. I told him about the family, as I do all the young ones when they get to be six.'

" 'An' what's he been tellin' you?' Th' ma's voice was sharp, worried, an' th' kid, he got real scairt.

"Th' ol' man laft a wheezy laf an' said, 'Oh, I asked him to tell me his stories. I have not been so cheered in many and many a year.

" 'Don't be hard on him, our Mary. Now that he's six, he knows the difference between real and make-believe. Remember, lass, the lad has never thought of them as lies because they were so real to him. Now, he knows he may tell them if he does not expect that people will believe them. He's too old to expect that anymore. He's been telling me he'd remember and not do that thing that worries you and makes you angry.'

"Th' boy's ma, she relaxt some. 'Da,' she said, 'if you can make him do that, I'll be so grateful to you. He's worried the life out of me with his imaginings.'

"Th' gramps looked over at th' boy. 'Now, then, our Ed. Do you give me your solemn promise, as God is your judge, that you'll never tell your tales to anyone—and expect them to believe you? That you'll stop worrying your good mother this way?'

"Th' kid thumped offa th' bench an' stood in fronta his gramps. 'I promise,' he said.

"Th' ol' man's wet eyes looked tearier than ever, but th' boy, he didn't mind now.

" 'Then all's well,' th' ol' man wheezed.

" 'Next week again, Mary?' th' ol' man said to his son's son's wife.

"Th' boy looked up at his ma an' tried t' tell her he wanted t' come again. In spite of her worry, she was a good ma, an' she got th' message. She took th' boy's hand and squeezed it, gentle-like.

128

" 'If you like, Da,' she said. 'Our Ed can come talk to you while I do the marketing.'

"Th' ol' man nodded. 'That's good,' he said.

"Th' kid walked right up to his gramps, put his arms aroun' th' scrawny neck, an' kissed the ol', wrinkled, teary cheek. He whispered in th' ol' ear, 'Next rain, th' wall comes down right by th' stream.'

"His gramps gave him a hug back. 'That's my good lad,' he said. 'You'll make a fine man. 'Til we meet again, lad, God bless you—and good luck.'

"Th' boy never saw his gramps alive again. He wept bitterly when his ma tol' him that, before they'd even got home, his gramps's heart had stopped.

"Nobody blamed *him,* praise God. His ma even tol' 'im he'd helpt th' ol' man die happy, enjoyin' his tales and promisin' t' be a good lad.

"When they held the viewin' an' th' funeral an' th' wake, th' lad found out just how many relatives he really had—an' he th' youngest of all. He got hisself proper upset, and cried. But then, at a do like that, most of 'em did the same. He fell asleep in a corner. His ma, or some other good woman, threw a warm coat over him an' let him lay. He woke up t' th' sound of men talkin'.

" 'When they were layin' him out, did anyone think t' look for th' luck piece? You remember, th' medal his great-grandda got for savin' all th' men in th' mine disaster back in th' ol' country?'

"No one had. Th' men talked quietly, not makin' fun a' the clear-minded ol' gaffer's one odd way.

" 'He'd have liked to give it to one of us, but he didn't, did he?'

"None of the men had it.

" 'It should go in his pocket when he's laid in earth. Keep him company.'

" 'I wonder about the boy. D'y'think he has it?'

" 'If he does, it was a gift, an' Da wanted for him to. Maybe he found someone to pass the luck to.'

" 'Shall we see?'

" 'We shall not! That's Da's business—an' th' lad's. If he made the ol' man's passin' happier, he earned it.'

The prospector was silent for so long that Carson wondered if he was all right. He moved at last and opened his hand. On the scarred, rough palm lay a thick, flat circle of pure gold, the stamping long since worn away. Ed looked up, his gaze meeting Carson's.

"When my time comes, and that's not for many and many a year—in our family, we live almost forever"—Carson could sense a family saying in the words—"I'll not have to wait and wait and hope and hope."

The lump in Carson's throat was so huge that he could neither breathe nor swallow around it. He fought it for a moment, and when he thought he could speak without disgracing himself, he said, "May you live another hundred years, in health and strength. But when the time comes for you to pass the luck, I shall be there."

His own voice sounded like someone else's, someone with a Welsh accent and a lead tenor quality. He had given two solemn promises in his life. He would keep them both.

Ed nodded and put his lucky piece into his pocket. "And now, our Carson, they have had time to put all the blame on the two of us, and we'd best be off."

15

Carson shook his head. Ed had not led the other false deputies to the men at the mine entrance this morning. Had he even gone back to Rightway last night? He doubted it. Ed would not be with the men to go into the mine and discover that Carson must have died in the cave-in. Carson could not decide what would be most likely to happen, might be happening now. But . . .

"I can't just leave. I thought I could, but I can't. Caryl's there. Soon, she's going to get herself into terrible trouble." He tried to smile. "Sometimes the luck isn't all good."

"We cain't do nothing fer her now. Won't be long b'fore she's havin' sec'nt thoughts s' dark 'n' fearsome she won't cause no trouble fer quite a spell."

Carson thought it over. Probably, Ed was right. Tired as he was, he needed time to get strong enough to handle the trouble when it came. He grunted assent and stood up. "OK," he said, "but I hope it's not too far."

Ed laughed silently. "Woulda been, if you'da took th' ol' entrance. I filled in that tunnel years ago when I found a little streak that'd pay out fer one man who didn't mind workin'. That's when I opened up th' one you used. We're only a hoot n' a holler." He led the way.

"Ever *ridden* a mule?" he asked over his shoulder.

"Never," Carson admitted. "Or a horse."

"My grandda was a learned man," Ed said. "He'd a sayin' fer everythin'. He'd 'a' said, 'New experiences are the books in the library of life.' I'd say y' was about t' open a new one."

They dropped over an edge to find a good-sized mule, handsome for his species, awaiting them. Carson grimaced. But maybe actual riding would be less unpleasant than being carried like a sack of rocks.

On the whole, Carson decided, he'd take books. Mule-riding did not prove to be his forte. But with Ed striding along holding the lead rope, Stubborn's four legs saved Carson what he estimated as six or seven miles. They made a semicircle on a route that could be called a path only because Ed knew where he was going, and an occasional mule-shoe print showed he and Stubborn had come this way before. Surprising greenness suggested a source of water near the neat cabin.

"Only five miles down t' Rightway," Ed said as he helped Carson off Stubborn. "That way." A tilt of his head indicated where. "But I allus come in from t'other side. Never hurts t' let folks think yer where y' ain't, iffen y' don't want vis'ters.

"Sometime I'll show y' where y' kin watch from. Close enough, mebbe. We'll see."

The only thing about the next days that Carson found less than perfect was his growing uneasiness about Caryl. Otherwise, although he was used to a different diet and considerably greater cleanliness, he was both actively happy and quietly content. And he learned. From a man whose entire adult life had been spent in out-of-the-way places, principally alone, Carson learned how to manage. Sixteen hours a day, he soaked up facts, techniques, reasons, and Ed's realistic philosophy. Ed had sayings for every occasion or situation.

"Man's the biggest danger, here or anywhere. What call d' y' have t' be scairt of a dumb beast?"

"If y' ain't gonna eat it, don't kill it."

"People with any sense 'tall make their livin's doin' what they like best."

"Doin' nothin' about somethin' is makin' a choice."

"Never run *away;* always run *to.* An' y' better be danged sure what's there."

"Make yer own rules about th' way y' live. Eat when yer hungry; sleep when yer tired. Iffen it don't hurt nobody, that is."

Ed talked about plants and animals and finding water, and, and, and. Carson listened.

Only two subjects they never discussed. One was the luck. To do so would have been redundant. Each of them used his talents whenever he needed, openly and without concern. Carson knew that part of his sense of peace, which overrode even his deep worry, came from this. He could do things Ed couldn't, like prevent a falling rock from hitting him without having to move or duck. On his part, Ed could tell the composition of something hidden. No wonder he was able to make a living in an area other prospectors had long since given up. His talent, he said, was like dowsing—finding water, which he could do, too—only he found metals.

The other subject that never came up was Carson's life before the earthquake.

Rather as if he were a self-willed amnesiac, Carson's sense of belonging where he was, with Ed, became complete the first evening. Ed took a battered guitar down off the wall and went out to the front steps with it. The old fingers were still supple enough to show how well he had once played. He began to sing. He had once had a true Welsh voice, and still it was true in both pitch and expression, only a little degraded in quality. Carson sang along. His voice didn't break often, and only when he pushed. Ed gave him a suggestion, now and then, about using it correctly, and to Carson's joy, Ed assured him that he'd sing like a Welshman once his voice settled.

Carson's memories of singing were all happy. His earliest remembrances were of the old lullabies and baby songs his father sang to him when he was little. On the few precious days when he and his father had time together alone, they always sang. The best of the few good times at Rightway were sing-alongs. Caryl, too, loved to sing. Carson could be at peace as long as there was music.

After a few days, Ed went alone to the lookout. Because he and Carson did not know whether the gang leader and his men were still in the area, he would not allow Carson to accompany him. When he returned, he assured Carson that nothing seemed changed. Carson knew Caryl was still in Rightway, still controlling herself, and he was content.

He felt so comfortable that when Ed took off alone for

the "ol' workin's" he was checking out—having exhausted all those in this area—Carson spent the days happily puttering about, "learnin' t' do fer hisself."

By the end of the second week, Carson knew a crisis was coming. Why Caryl had held off this long was beyond him. Perhaps she'd been too scared.

He voiced his question to Ed.

"I have been thinking about this," Ed said. The longer Carson stayed, the more Welsh Ed sounded. Carson realized he, too, spoke with the melody, the word choice, and the distinctive articulations. "It has come to me that you feel what your sister feels. If this is so, perhaps she senses your emotions. You are at peace. Is it so, you know what she feels?"

"I do," Carson verified. "That is how I tell when she is likely to start . . . moving things. When I am near her, the luck tells me what and where and how powerfully. I can stop her."

"Can you, now?" Ed peered at him sharply.

Carson nodded.

"And what else can you do?"

Carson started to say, "That's all," but he stopped. The morning after the quake, when he'd become so angry . . . he didn't know what it was, but he had done something that had prevented Caryl from speaking, then from striking the match. And later, the keys to the Cat and still later, the incident at the lunch counter.

"I do not know what else it is that I can do," he said slowly. "I was very angry when I did it."

Ed waited.

Ed's waits were precious to Carson. If he wanted to speak, Ed wanted to listen. If he did not, Ed did not want to hear.

This time, because he wanted to tell someone, someone who would not judge but might be able to help—Ed—he explained as much as he could.

Ed said nothing at all for several minutes.

"Do you think you could do it if you were not angry?" he asked.

"Just stop her from moving or speaking because I believed she shouldn't?"

"Or someone else. Me, for example."

"I don't know," Carson said. "Maybe. But not just like that. Not just . . . do it. It's something I *have* to do. If you were going to—to put your hand on a rattler, I know I'd try."

"Do you think you would succeed?"

"I don't know. Maybe it's only Caryl, because she's my sister."

Ed nodded. "At some time in the future, you must find out. Where, under what circumstances, with whom, I cannot guess, but you cannot go on through life not knowing."

Carson agreed. "There used to be a place, a university somewhere, where a Professor Rhine did experiments with things like this, but he died a long time ago. I don't know if anybody else is working on it."

"I have heard of someone else, but I cannot remember the name. English, no doubt." A hundred years an American, Ed would still distrust the English. "An organization. You will have to find it."

Carson stared at Ed. The word "organization" triggered a painful memory he did not want to recall. He winced and turned away.

Ed waited.

"When I was a lot younger," Carson said, hoping that if he talked it out, he might be able to get rid of it, "my mother got really excited about something in the paper. She called my father at work, long distance. She'd read a feature article on the Logran Organization, how it was putting a lot of money into research on psi and ESP phenomena and talents. Mother wanted to get in touch with them and see if they could help us with Caryl.

"Dad told her he'd check it out, to wait until he got home. That's the part I don't like to think about."

Ed busied himself about dinner preparation.

"Dad got back two days late. He and Mother had—well, I guess you'd call it a fight. They yelled at each other, and they never had. Mother said it was a chance. Dad said he'd found out we'd be experimental animals and might end up mind-damaged. Several children had. He would not let that happen to us. If Mother so much as wrote a letter, he'd have her declared an incurable alcoholic or insane or something before he'd let that bunch get their hands on us. He'd deny everything, dope Caryl—he'd find something that'd turn her off—and do whatever he had to do to keep me from talking. If she made him do that to his . . . to his son . . . he wouldn't be able to live with her. He'd hate her, and he'd hate himself worse."

"Then I do not think you should go near the Logran Organization," Ed said with such deceptive mildness that Carson's bad mood broke, and he snorted with amusement. "I knew I was right," the old man continued. "Never trust the English."

The remark was such a non sequitur that Carson burst out laughing.

"You may laugh," Ed said with what sounded like seriousness, but Carson knew was not, "but your father would have said the same."

The last was serious. Carson did not correct the tense. Everything else, he would tell Ed. That his parents lived and probably were searching for him and Caryl, he would not tell.

He had completely forgotten the note.

16

Caryl lay on the boardlike mattress between the rough-dried, sweet-smelling sheets, and shook. She could not stop shaking. Her hands and feet were icy, sweaty lumps. She could hardly move her fingers and toes. Her face, conversely, burned as if with fever, and trickles of moisture slid down her temples and soaked into the too-soft pillow. Her skin hurt. Every seam on the muslin nightdress dug channels into her flesh. No way she turned seemed to eliminate them all. Even her hair had become an enemy. She could smell the fear-sweat.

She knew she was going to die and go straight to hell. Her heart raced so violently, so erratically, that she was convinced it was beating her to death. In a terrified totality of agony, she knew she deserved to die. She could repeat and repeat, "I had to, I had to," until her tongue split into a thousand clanging bell-clappers. But below the level of Caryl, Caryl, Caryl, by which she had always lived, the knowledge and understanding of what she had done had untombed a conscience. Like a speaking zombie, it replied, "You killed him. You killed Carson. You killed your brother. You are Cain. You will go branded all your life."

She rubbed an icy hand across her forehead. Surely the burning-red C would be branded so deeply that she could feel it. Nothing but skin, smooth skin. She longed to proclaim her guilt publicly, to tear a huge, gory letter with her nails, to punish herself, if no one else would. The demon of self-preservation that had made her scream out the accusations against Carson balled her fingers into fists and shoved the hands under the covers.

She fought the demon, her mind and body a battleground between two forces, neither of which was Caryl.

If she could only cry! But witches can't cry. From her earliest memories the sound of her mother's drunken voice wailed in self-pity and pronounced her daughter *witch*. "See, she screams and yells and kicks and claws, but never cries. Not a tear. Not one tear on that angry, ugly, red little face. A witch. A baby witch. I've given birth to a witch." In her drunkenness, Mother had forgotten that Carson was tearless, too. On some level Caryl knew this, but what she remembered was her mother's conviction that she, Caryl, was a witch.

Mother had said much more, the alcohol releasing her tongue to speak her fear and despair. Caryl's mind had retained only these phrases, grinding them deeper and deeper into permanent grooves in her brain, permanent background to all her thoughts.

Jane came into the room. She observed Caryl with the compassionate objectivity all these adults had. Caryl squeezed her eyes shut, willing the woman to go away, to leave her alone. Or—*please, please, God*—to come over and hold her, or *anything*. The woman turned and left the room. In a moment or so, she was back.

"Here. Sit up and drink this."

She's being as kind as she knows how, said one part of Caryl's internal dialogue.

She's going to poison you, you killer, said the other. Caught between the two, Caryl's body froze.

Jane sighed. Caryl could hear a slight thud as Jane set something on the floor.

In less than half a minute, Caryl had been hauled upright, her jaws pried open, and a warm bitter drink poured into her mouth.

"Swallow or sleep in the stink for a week," Jane's voice told her.

Caryl swallowed.

Three minutes later, she was asleep.

When she woke, she was woozy. The drugged sleep had contained ghastly nightmares. Her sick, frightened, beaten mind tried to hold onto them. Her will, utterly helpless, could not send them back into the unreality of dream.

Caryl stumbled out of bed and groped under it for the chamber pot. The room was bitterly cold, the low temperature of the mountain nights not yet alleviated by dawn and the brilliant, searing sunshine. If she wet her nightgown, she'd wet the sheets. One got new nightwear for the body and bed once a week. She'd have to sleep in her own urine. Caryl pulled the narrow gown up around her waist, bunching it high in front. Gooseflesh pimpled her legs and lower body. She shivered so violently that she could hardly squat. The edge of the china pot was so cold that it burned, and she could feel it rock. Her urine scalded her. The odor was enough to make her gag. No toilet tissue, either. Just hard, scratchy pages from a mail-order catalog. To soften it, she'd have to crumple and rub it. One hand still clutched the nightgown. Caryl swallowed tears of frustration and misery and ineptitude.

She couldn't just squat here forever! Her bottom was freezing to the pot, and her shaking would soon overturn it. Caryl reached down into her reservoir of power—only to find it so drained that she could not draw up even enough to soften the paper. In utter defeat, she curled a toe over the remains of the catalog, tore off a sheet, and swiped at herself. It helped little, but it was all she could do.

Not until she was back in the cold bed did she realize that the pot was still uncovered and right out in the narrow passageway between her bed and that of the next girl. Still sobbing, she reached out and pulled it over. No. She could still smell it. She got up, found the lid, set it clattering on the pot, and pushed the disgusting apparatus back under the bed.

By now, she should have been wide-awake, if dreadfully cold, but Jane had poured an adult dose of the sleeping draught down her throat. In a moment she slept again, curled into the smallest ball she could make of her bony, angular body.

Not until she woke again—pushing covers away and aware of sweat running down her face and sides and thighs— did it occur to her that for the first time in her life she had done an unpleasant, difficult, disgusting task entirely by using her body.

She sat up, furious. She was alone in the room. "It's all Carson's fault," she whispered through clenched teeth. "If he hadn't brought me here . . ."

Saying Carson's name bathed her in fulminating acid.

She had killed Carson as surely as if she'd cut his throat. She had sent him out with those men. To die.

In the mental acid-bath, stripped of all illusions and justifications, she could no longer pretend Carson had brought her here. He hadn't. He had recognized, way back at the train station, that something was wrong. She knew then that he'd wanted her to come with him, to jump on the train, to get away. He could have gone, maybe, by himself. He had stayed to try to help her.

Now there was no one to help her.

Caryl sat and rocked. Back and forth, back and forth, the rhythm of her mother's heart before she was born a witch.

Jane walked in. "Time to be up and dressed," she said.

Caryl rocked.

Jane sighed, stepped over, and yanked Caryl out of bed and onto her feet. "Slugabeds go hungry," the woman said. "Get dressed, comb your hair, empty the pot, wash, then come to the kitchen. I'll have some bread and milk for you." She left the room.

The world outside Caryl's head became all too real again. She did as she was bidden. She did not think about it. She tried not to think about anything.

Sitting by herself in the almost empty kitchen, Caryl spooned up a mouthful of her breakfast. Homemade wholegrain bread and warm goat's milk tasted dreadful, as it always had. This morning, she could not bear it.

"May I have a little sugar, please?" she said, trying not to gag. Sometimes, if she sounded abject enough, one of these people would let her have something a little like it was before.

"Sugar do not be good for children," Jane said. "Your teeth be a mass of fillings. Now that you live on a healthful diet, you have not developed one cavity. Certainly, for you, sugar be very bad."

The simple statement, the explanation, shattered Caryl wide open. She helped herself to the sugar.

Jane watched the top fly off the rarely opened canister, and the loosely packed ball of sugar rise out, float over, and rain into Caryl's bowl. She stepped to the table, picked up the bowl, and removed it. Caryl snatched for it with her mind, but the woman's grip was strong.

"I want it. It's mine!" Caryl screamed.

Jane poured the meal into the sink.

Caryl picked up the bowl as Jane released it. She threw it, stunningly hard, at Jane's head.

Jane ducked. The bowl shattered.

Caryl's shirt over her head, her trousers and underpants around her knees, she was spanked for the second time in her life. She kicked and screamed and vomited with pain and fury.

When it was over, she washed, changed her clothes, scrubbed the floor, and picked up every piece of broken bowl. She washed out her garments and Jane's and hung them on a line outside to dry.

Then she had a second, sugarless, bowl of bread and milk.

She was taken to her isolation room and told to remain there during lunch. Her behavior was so unacceptable that others should not have to associate with her. If she did as she was told, she might eat later. Jane would put her portion aside.

That afternoon, Pastor entered her cell. He brought with him the long, thin, whiplike cane he used to chastise children who strayed from The Way or failed to learn it with sufficient rapidity or commitment. He laid it to one side. Then he began questioning.

Caryl was unable to keep anything from him. He seemed to know if she lied or evaded. At first, he only probed deeper, frightening her but not hurting her. Failing to obtain the answers he wanted, he took up the cane.

"I be not a believer in striking children," he said, "and those who be raised rightly rarely need it. But you, who did be raised in total neglect of all your parents should have taught you . . . If you be able to respond only to pain, you will have to feel it."

By the end of another hour, Caryl had confessed not only to what she had done, but also to a hundred other things of which he accused her and she agreed in order to prevent that slashing whip from cutting her again. She was utterly defeated.

Pastor rose and looked down at her, judgment in his whole demeanor. "Never again will you use those talents of the Devil in your own behalf. You will use them only when I tell you to, and only in ways I command. In time, you will have worked yourself into a state of emptiness, of grace. When you can no longer be used by Satan to do his works, you will accept The Way freely."

He might force her to do what he told her to. He might keep her from using her powers for herself. But he would never, never, make her accept The Way freely—not even if he succeeded in freeing her of telekinesis. Caryl knew she would die first.

Her body healed, and she would not even have scars. Her mind did not. The power grew until, almost, she had enough to . . . to bring down the buildings around her tormentor and captor . . . and run, run into the desert— to that mine, maybe, and lose herself there. Anything would be better than this.

He knew exactly when to begin his orders. Jane rousted her out of bed at five-thirty one cold, dark morning. Pastor put Caryl to work. She built much of their new church. He worked her to total exhaustion, until she dropped, and his little cane could not make her rise again. A day to recuperate, then back at it. He knew exactly how far to go. She settled into a pattern of mindless effort, mindless relaxation, deathlike sleep. But she was not accepting. *One day, one day, one day,* she thought, never finishing the sentence. She did not dare. Somehow, he knew.

17

The day Caryl was beaten into submission was almost equally horrible for Carson. He was unusually sleepy all morning, yawning his way from sleeping bag to front porch and back again. Ed observed him but said little.

When Caryl began to react to something with fear and fury and frustration and all of the emotions Carson knew preceded her worst bouts of magic, the boy woke. He paced.

"What bothers you, lad?" Ed asked.

"It's Caryl. She's building up. Something's going to happen. I've got to stop it."

"Why?" Ed asked.

Carson spouted everything he felt, everything he knew,

all the pent-up experiences of controlling Caryl so she wouldn't end up killing or maiming someone who'd angered her. He told Ed what *The Book of The Way* taught about those who had special talents.

When the whip slashed down for the first time, Carson reacted as Caryl had. He screamed.

Through a red haze of shock and pain and total fury, Carson realized he was trying to get out the door, and Ed was preventing him. He fought.

Ed, thick, solid-muscled, gnarled and dried by years and desert, held Carson as the boy used to hold Caryl. He did not fight back, but controlled Carson so the boy could not hurt him.

"I've got to go help her!" Carson yelled. "It has to be Pastor. He's hurting her! She's too little to fight him."

Carson fought Ed as hard as Caryl resisted Pastor, and as ineffectively. He was completely exhausted by the end of the session.

When the worst was over, and Caryl was slathered with salve and put to bed, Carson went out like a light and slept for twenty-four hours.

He woke realizing that Ed had prevented him from throwing himself headlong into the same trap Caryl was in. If he were to reappear in Rightway, neither he nor Caryl would ever emerge from Pastor's grasp.

Caryl was not dead or even crippled. She hurt, but she was being cared for. Nevertheless, he must do something.

Ed was not in the cabin and did not reappear until the following morning.

Carson rushed out to meet him. "Can't you at least call the sheriff, the real one, from the station?" he begged Ed.

"Where do you think I have been?" Ed said. "I went down as soon as you were asleep. The line has been cut,

148

likely when the false sheriff led his men elsewhere. I do not know how soon the repair people will come to fix it. Probably, they will not even know. In the five years the phone has been there, I do not suppose it has been used more than two or three times."

"What about going down to Rightway and finding out about Caryl?"

"Do you think they would let me get closer to her than I did the first time?"

Carson didn't.

"Well, can't we go to the station and take a train to wherever the sheriff's office is?"

Ed looked at Carson for a time, then went on caring for Stubborn. "Son," he said at last, "we must take things slowly. I have thought about this matter all the way down and back. As long as you continue to receive signals from your sister, she may not be well and happy, but she is alive.

"Pastor is a driven man. He does not admit to himself that he feels guilt for your death, but he does. What he allowed to happen to you gave a terrible shock to the Followers. They are good people. I know them well enough to be sure they feel desperate guilt and shame. They will allow him to force Caryl to use her powers for his purposes, but they will not stand by and permit him to kill again."

"But he tortured her!"

"Caned her, I should think, exactly as he would any of the other children who disobeyed him. They will accept that, so long as she is not permanently damaged—and that, they will not allow.

"He is too intelligent and perceptive a man not to be well aware of his followers' attitudes. He will take great care not to step beyond the point at which they will cease to follow him. He will be in a state of great tension and wariness. We must think, plan, and prepare before we act."

At the month's end, they decided, Ed would sling the pack saddle and his bags of ore—mostly rocks—on Stubborn's back and take off for the commune, then the railroad. He would set the signals at Rightway Station. The daily local would stop for him. He and the trainmen were old cronies, and they always let Stubborn ride in the baggage car, as long as Ed didn't mind riding there, too. They met whenever Ed went to Jackson, a veritable metropolis in comparison with Rightway, two stops to the north. In Jackson, Ed would talk to the real sheriff, also a friend. He would pass on any pertinent observations he had made at Rightway and pick up any information he could.

Carson was sufficiently familiar with the area and the few things he must do at the cabin that he felt comfortable about being alone. He was getting tired of living off the land, as they had done in order not to alert others he was with Ed. Even canned peaches and boiled pinto beans would taste good. Snake and ground squirrel and jackrabbit and the wild, edible plants had supplied most of their meals for the last weeks. Consequently, he could now snare, gut, skin, and cook acceptably.

Carson felt quietly optimistic. Since that one awful day, his signals from Caryl had a soothing regularity. One day of rest, one day of sustained, controlled use of her ability. Whatever happened that day obviously set up this pattern, and Caryl was not using her power to harm or control others. He felt that she was being controlled, although not in the ways he could do so. Maybe somebody was doing a better job than he'd done, and Caryl was all right.

Certainly, Carson no longer twinged early every other

morning when he knew Caryl was using her talent. His own activities were so completely satisfying and filled with so much he needed—learning and acceptance and a growing relationship with the old man—that Caryl receded more and more from his consciousness. On her rest days he actually forgot her. In learning, with Ed's help, to control his reaction to Caryl's telekinesis, he learned to blunt his acute knowledge of her emotions. At last, he experienced again the freedom of the moments after the earthquake. Having never been free, Carson appreciated freedom and buttressed it against every intellectual realization he had. Remembering the kind of person who now controlled Caryl would cause him pointless suffering. Pointless, as Ed finally made him understand, because a thirteen-year-old boy and a very old man could do little against an entire community—particularly one with a God-given Gift to know and to practice The One and Only Right Way.

They must get help, and to do so would take time. Time, at first, seemed Carson's enemy, but Ed could not change his habits of years without causing people to wonder why. They might answer that question by wondering if perhaps Carson's body did not lie under that great rockfall in the mine. Once Carson accepted the necessity to wait, the waiting itself became his greatest treasure.

Before he left, Ed sat on the front steps with Carson and shifted back into the old prospector as he talked. "I'm goin' t' Rightway first," he said. "Pick up th' ore they're holdin' fer me. See iffen yer sister's happy. Iffen she is, you ain't got no cause t' fret yer head about her. Iffen she ain't—well, that's one a th' things I'll say t' Sheriff Tait. Won't be back fer a week. Only if I'm not back in two weeks do y' git worrit. An' then, y' don't go down there—" a tilt of his head toward Rightway—"no matter if yer sister is there. Y' git yerself t' Jacks'n." The old man pulled out a small leather bag and dug around in it, bringing up a twenty-dollar bill. "This here's mor'n enough fer fare an' food an' a bed at the Y. Go see Sheriff Tait. Iffen he ain't seen me fer a dog's age, tell 'im t' call out th' Marines 'r anybody else'll come." Ed handed Carson a folded sheet of lined yellow paper. "This here's fer Jase—th' sheriff—so's he'll know y' come from me.

"Y' sure y' know th' landmarks—where I put th' water?"

One of the first things they had done was to ensure that Carson, should he ever have to, could get to the station. He could make it in two long hikes, holing up to sleep in a place Ed had described. Ed's trail did not come within sight of the road to Rightway until the last few miles.

Carson thought each landmark, remembered every detail Ed had told him. "I can make it," he said. "I hope I don't have to."

Ed slapped him on the shoulder. "Not much chance. When them city fellers took off, we lost mosta th' problem, even though they did cut th' phone line. Only thing y' got t' be wary of is rattlers—an' y' got high boots, thick pants, two good eyes, two good ears, an' a snakestick."

"And the Followers," Carson muttered.

"Think that Pastor'd let 'em go down to th' railway any day but Friday? Y' keep markin' that calendar, so's you start no later 'n Tuesd'y. That'll give y' plenty a' time."

"OK," Carson agreed.

Carson waited for Ed without a sense of haste. He knew Ed would not find Caryl to be happy. He regretted it. His life would be so much simpler if Caryl were out of it permanently. She had hated Rightway as much as—or perhaps more than—he. The possibility that she was now happy in Rightway did not exist. He determined to revel in what were likely to be his last days of liberty.

Ed had told Carson what Caryl was doing—or what Ed assumed she must be doing. Carson had Ed's permission to go to the lookout—now that the men who had taken him to the mine had been gone for some weeks—to watch the progress. Carson set off with the field glasses the morning after Ed left. Today was a workday for Caryl. The almost half-finished church declared itself to be her work. In no other way could it have grown so fast. Had it not been obvious to Carson with what anguish Caryl performed her task, he might have felt jealous of her ability.

Carson gritted his teeth. When he and Caryl got together again, could he control her? She had learned so much, become so powerful! He shook.

"I'll leave her there forever before I let her make me a slave again," he vowed.

He couldn't, and even as he made the promise, he knew it. If Ed said Caryl was miserable, he'd have to tell Ed that their parents were alive, let him get in touch with Dad, and make his own way elsewhere. Ed might even let him come back after Dad had come, rescued Caryl, and gone. Going home with Caryl was out. No matter how much he loved his parents, they'd allowed Caryl to dominate him for years. He could see no other possibility for the future.

Two days later, at daybreak, Carson slung on his knapsack and closed the cabin. He left the signals he and Ed had agreed upon should he be off hiking when Ed returned. With food for a week, both his canteen and one of Ed's waterskins, the belt-knife Ed had given him, and his snakestick, he felt competent to spend a few nights away from the cabin. He wanted the openness of the desert sky, the emptiness of the desert scene, even the bitter cold of the desert night. There, he could go in memory when things got bad again. He had become, partly because Ed set him such a clear example, a total realist. "Yesterday, lad, is

153

valuable only for what it taught you. Tomorrow is worthwhile only because, God willing, you will live another day. Today is the only day of your life. Make it a good one." Realism did not require anticipation of future unhappiness, only active participation in the present. He would make of his few days the best present he could.

18

Carson left the cabin well before eight o'clock, in the still cold early sunshine, and hiked with his shadow as a pointer ahead of him. He would go up through the high pass and look westward across the world. He knew he was too far inland, but would he imagine he saw any results of the earthquake? More practically, Ed had told him where he'd gone the days Carson did for himself. Another abandoned mine lay in a valley he could hike into from the pass. Interesting place, Ed said, with a ghost town nobody else had discovered yet. When the matter of Caryl was settled, Ed planned to move there. He'd rebuild one of the houses and continue living as he always had, chipping out the tiny threads of silver left behind as not worth the time and effort to mine. Ed thought Carson might enjoy "pokin' aroun'," but he'd asked Carson to take reasonable care—and not to go into the mine. While the luck would protect him, the amount of damage he could do, should his presence disturb things before Ed got his props and braces in, might make it much more difficult—or even impossible—to work the streak. He wouldn't go in, but he had told Ed that he wanted to see the town.

The bones of the land spoke to his feet, to his body, and he made excellent progress.

Carson found a sheltered spot to camp for the night, made a tiny fire, ate, and settled down to watch the stars and listen to the night sounds. In the morning, he cleaned up and went on, cold, alone, and happy in a way he could not quite understand. Actively happy, as if . . . He shut off his mind and enjoyed.

He spent the next night just over the crest of the pass, in a rocky cavelet from which he could see down into the valley. The town lay around a bend from his vantage point, the mine still farther away, so he could see neither. The valley was not one he would have chosen to enter, had Ed not told him what he would find. The only sign that humans had ever been in this canyon was the barely discernible trace of an old road. It curved around the bend from the town, straightened along the floor of the gulch, then zigzagged up the steep slope on the western side. As Carson's viewpoint was on the east, it'd be a long way around, if he decided to take the road down. Ed said he needn't, that with the luck he could descend safely from this point. He looked forward to morning and discovering the hidden places for himself.

He was more tired than he realized. Not until sunlight spilled over the crest—*It must be after ten o'clock!* he thought—

did he waken. Lazily eating handfuls of raisins and nuts, he waited until the sun warmed the area a little more. He had no schedule. If he stayed here all day, it wouldn't matter. Ed couldn't be back before Saturday, and Carson had left the signals. He faced the fact that he didn't want to go back at all. Going back meant Caryl, and eventually facing Dad with what he'd done, and having to admit everything to Ed. He'd constructed his own prison, and he had no desire to watch its door close and lock behind him.

A strange idea occurred to him. Had Ed once felt like this—and made the decision not to go back? Maybe he had. He seemed to understand too well for someone who'd never . . .

Maybe he *could* live with Ed. He was happier here than he'd ever been, learning a lot, enough to be really useful soon. And he had the luck.

He wiggled around so he could see down into the valley—and froze stiff in surprise. A jeep racketed along the road from the ghost town! Jeeps all look alike, but Carson knew he'd seen that one before. So this was where the kidnappers had gone! They must have been smarter than Ed realized; somehow they, too, had found the ghost town—a perfect place to make their headquarters. They must have moved in sometime after Ed had last been there, some two weeks before.

The men in the jeep couldn't possibly spot him, so Carson felt in no danger, but he did wonder where they were going. In a minute or two, the station wagon followed the jeep around the bend and up the switchback. Were all the men gone? Possibly. Probably. But if he went down, he'd have to be careful.

He would go down. This was his last chance at an adventure, his last chance to do something that might help to make up for—for the awful things that were happening to Caryl because he hadn't been able to rescue her. If he could make sure this was the same band of men who thought they had killed him . . . Carson had no doubt that they were at least among the looters and killers the radio and the PA announcements had warned about, long ago near the end of his previous life. . . . If he could make certain of that, get out safely, and pass the word to the authorities, he'd have done something he could be proud of.

Carson moved slowly and carefully, trusting the luck and keeping in the shadows for the most part. When he reached the bottom, he did not take the road, but followed the foot of the cliff, a longer but less obvious path. He came to the bend and checked carefully before making the turn. Somebody lived there. He saw smoke from a chimney—and on a hilltop above, an antenna.

Um-hm. They had to have a way of monitoring the police and sheriff's bands. Ed had said he thought they had a powerful radio transceiver in the back of the station wagon. Carson had felt sure before. Now he was positive. A radio meant that he also had a method of communicating, if he could figure out a way to use it. He had his CB license, and a more complicated rig shouldn't be too hard to work.

A man opened a door, walked out onto a porch, and looked around, not as if he were looking for anything in particular, but as if he'd had enough of indoors. Carson willed him back into the house, but the man stumped off the porch and walked slowly down the road toward the mine.

Carson waited until the man had been gone for some five minutes, then moved across the empty area swiftly but without running. He breathed a sigh of relief when he stood against the shaky side of a house far more decrepit than the two the men had taken over. He peeked around a corner. He could see the entrance to the mine. It once had been a far larger operation than the small mine in which the men had tested Carson.

The man did not reappear, and Carson felt at a loss. He had no plans and must make some. First, he'd better take a look into those houses. Maybe something there could prove the men's identities to the authorities.

Sneaking around while wearing a backpack didn't seem too smart. He unslung his and stuck his head through a glassless window of the house behind which he sheltered. Not a bad spot. The pack would be unnoticeable but easy to retrieve. He set it inside.

He'd be less apparent if he approached the houses from the back, but the man could return without Carson's being aware of him. He chose this route, but checked the road before he tried to peer into the house. What was the man doing in the mine? Whatever it was, Carson didn't see how it could take long. He'd better hurry.

The first house had been clumsily repaired, indifferently cleaned, and apparently was used for sleeping and eating. The next house, from which the man had come, must have the radio. Carson looked up, wondering if the radio required a wire from the antenna to the set. Modern ones didn't, but who knew?

No wire. He checked the road again. Good thing. The man was more than halfway back to the houses. Carson rushed quietly to a window. Yes. The transceiver sat on a camp table. He slid around to the back of the building and listened. Now, if the man only would go into the other house.

No such luck. The man entered the building behind which Carson hid. The house had no windows on this side, so while the man could not see him, neither could Carson see in. Should he chance creeping around to the side again?

He waited. Maybe the man was going to turn on the radio. Would he use earphones—Carson had seen a set— or would he just turn on the speaker?

"Lessee if she's on again. It's about time," the man said.

A woman's voice, rich and melodious, a voice Carson's instincts would have said to trust if it had told him to pet a coiled rattlesnake, dropped the world out from under the boy's feet as even the earthquake had not done.

"I speak for the Logran Organization," the woman said.

Carson had not gotten rid of it by telling Ed about the Logran Organization's experimentation on children. Remembering it, speaking of it, had revitalized his deathly dread of being in the power of such people.

"We seek two children, one approximately twelve to fourteen, the other, say eight to ten. The younger one is a powerful telekinetic who totally lacks self-control. The older one probably is not telekinetic, but can control the younger one so that she will not harm others."

How can she know? Carson thought. *She can't. Somebody had to tell her.*

"We have received information from a road crew near the disaster area. These men tell us the younger one is a girl, Caryl, the older, a boy, Carson."

Carson ground his teeth. The road crew must have advertised everything they knew. He hated them.

The voice continued. "We have narrowed the locus of psionic power to an almost uninhabited area in the northern desert."

How could they? For the first time, Carson was forced to consider that the Logran Organization might have people who actually could locate them. He kept listening, hoping the *real* explanation would come, as it had before.

"We know the children are there, and that their problems are rising to a climax."

She must be using that as a hook. He knew how near Caryl was to blowing, but how could anybody else? Just a gimmick!

"For some reason we do not know, the children have been separated. This and cruel physical and psychological treatment of the girl are precipitating a crisis so potentially destructive that the Organization is using every available method of communication: every radio and television network, law enforcement agency, newspaper, magazine, ham operator in the area—even the National Guard and the Army—to get the news out."

Carson's sense of total helplessness had never been so deep. People with that kind of money—and, more important, that kind of influence! What could he do, even with Ed's help, even if he got in touch with Dad? He ached with the unfairness, with overwhelming frustration. *Like trying to fight a flood with a teaspoon,* he thought.

"We care about these children and all others who face life with psi characteristics other people do not understand. Because Caryl can do nothing else to free herself from the torture she endures, we care that she will kill. We will not allow that to happen if anything we can do will prevent it. Her trauma must stop!"

With the last statement, Carson could agree, and his concurrence startled him.

"At the least, the controller must be returned to the uncontrolled."

Sure, get us both at the same time, Carson responded silently, hating her, hating them all, knowing their caring for what it really was—a determination to enslave Caryl and himself.

"The children *must be located* so they can be helped. The Logran Organization is the only agency that can offer this help. Please believe me! We do know more about psi functions, their use and control, than does any other individual or group in the world—certainly than anyone in this country."

I'll bet you do, Carson thought. He ached for all those poor kids they'd experimented on, leaving them like vegetables, probably. Exactly as he and Caryl would be if those demons-in-human-form succeeded in their intent.

"We are offering rewards varying from ten thousand to one million dollars for verifiable information about the location of either or both of the children. The exact amounts depend upon the nature and usefulness of the information. We will pay these rewards only if the children are alive and totally unharmed."

Unharmed? Of course! Any harm would come from the experiments conducted by the Logran Organization.

Oh, God! He and Caryl were the subjects of the most intense search ever known! The media, the military, even amateurs—the Logran Organization had everyone looking for them.

Horrified, Carson knew now exactly where the men in the jeep and the station wagon had gone this morning in such a rush: to kidnap Caryl and turn her over to the mind-destroyers.

Then they would search for him. They would return to the old mine to make certain he was dead, and when they found no body . . .

Oh, God, Carson prayed, *they're buying us. For that much money, anybody'd sell us into slavery! Don't let them. Don't let them.*

Even people dedicated to preventing the exploitation of

children could salve their consciences by believing the reasons given by the woman on the radio.

"Please, please, do not consider this the message of a crank or a psychotic," she said. "Psi characteristics exist. They are both natural to the human species and normal to the individuals who have them. Uncontrolled, they can wreak great harm. Self-controlled, used in the ways we have learned and are learning to use them, they are of great value. Help us to find and help these children. Give us the information, and we will take it from there."

Take us straight to hell! Carson could hardly think anymore. More than he wanted to live, he wanted to get his hands around the throat making all those beautiful sounds, saying such persuasive words and meaning such horrible things.

"Do not attempt to handle this situation—or take advantage of it—yourself," the woman continued. "If you force them to defend themselves, you may bring serious danger to yourselves and others, for they are children, and the younger one is alone, terrified, and under unbearable stress. She trusts no one but her brother, whom we believe she thinks dead."

How could they know that? No one could have told them—the kidnappers certainly wouldn't have sent any information until Caryl was safely in their hands. Rightway didn't have a radio or any other form of communication with the outside world. The last person on earth who would give them away was Ed, and he was the only other person who knew.

"If you're listening, Carson or Caryl, or both of you, please, please, get back together as fast as you can. Caryl, hold on. Please hold on. Don't let whatever's made you so desperate force you to let go. Carson, find her! Find her fast! Our strongest empath says you doubt your ability to control Caryl. Do *not!* Your recent experiences have strengthened you, although in ways you may not recognize as strength. You can! You must!"

I will, witch. I will soon. And not in the way you expect. Even you can't find out something from non-telepaths.

"Does anyone out there know these children, does anyone who loves them seek them? If you doubt our motives because you have heard of the Organization's research into psi functions in the past, please listen. All such activities ceased upon the death of the former head of the Organization. We who share the leadership now beg you to learn what the present House of Logran offers. Get in touch with us. Pick up a phone and call Information. Help us to help your children!"

Dad! Don't. Don't believe her. You know what they are! You'd have committed Mother as insane to keep us out of their hands. Don't believe her! Carson wanted to cry, but all he could do was listen.

But if there was more, Carson did not hear it. The man inside the house shut off the radio.

"We'll at least get the girl for you, lady," the man gloated. "For that much cash I'd sell my own kids, if I had any." He laughed.

Of all the sounds in the universe, perhaps only that one—the sound of cynical, disparaging, exultant laughter—could have brought Carson out of his personal hell. Anger replaced terror. Fury conquered dread. Rage, white rage, turned Carson into himself—and into something quite distant from himself. He sat up, breathed deeply, slowed his heartbeat, and *thought.*

19

The best opportunity—for himself and Caryl—was the one the gang was providing. The men had gone to Rightway to kidnap Caryl and bring her back here. This was a workday, and she would be demonstrating her telekinesis, so they could have no doubt of her identity. Carson hoped the men would not kill too many of the Followers, but in his present state he was unable to care much if they did.

When they had her here, drugged, the leader would communicate with the Logran Organization. Those people his father so despised, so hated, would arrive to remove her. Between the time she got here and the time the Organization did, Carson knew he had to take Caryl to a place the kidnappers and the Logran people would not dare to go.

They would go into the mine.

Only Ed could follow them there. Ed would not. If not before, Ed would hear the Organization's message when he got to Sheriff Tait's office in Jackson. Carson knew Ed would remember what Carson had told him about the Logran Organization. He would not let those people get them. He would go back to the cabin alone, find Carson's message about going hiking, and put two and two together correctly.

If Ed had already told the sheriff? If he was forced to communicate with the Organization? He would become the old prospector, be furious when he discovered Carson wasn't at the cabin. He would shake off the Organization and the law and come looking.

If Carson could bring Caryl out of the mine at some other place, Ed would find them and take them somewhere he knew to be safe. Ed would go to the nearest working telephone, put in an anonymous call, and Dad would come get them. Both of them.

Carson slipped away from the house so silently that an owl would never have known he stirred. He returned to the little cave at the top of the valley, lay prone, and waited.

This he did without realizing he had moved. His mind no longer accepted information from his senses regarding his physical surroundings. His body operated without needing such information, moving with a sureness he would perhaps never again experience.

Consciously, Carson tore down the barriers he had built in his mind between himself and his knowledge of Caryl— her whereabouts, her state of mind, the condition of her power-bank, his own warnings before she mind-moved. What he obtained was not telepathy, if he could believe

166

the little he knew about how telepathy worked, or clairvoyance or any other of the psi characteristics he had tried not to learn about. With the talents he did have and by applying intellect and intuition, he was able to follow the sequence of events.

Carson concentrated. He could be positive that the jeep and the station wagon raced along the Followers' road to Rightway. Then he seemed to tune in. Caryl and Pastor, concentrating intensely, did not become conscious of the vehicles until they were quite close. Caryl spotted them first. Her emotional burst affected not only Carson, but also Pastor. For an instant, the man was distracted. What could cause her to—

In that instant, Caryl exploded. With every dammed-up erg of her power, Caryl demolished the work she had been commanded to do. The half-finished church disintegrated as if struck with a giant wrecking ball. Wood and tiles and adobe bricks flew like missiles. Caryl, standing inviolate, laughed hysterically. She ran this way and that, shrieking and screaming, evading the hands of the few Followers who, still on their feet, tried to capture her. Pastor, grazed by bricks and bowled over by the blast, struggled to his feet. He must have raised his whip, for Carson caught a sense of additional triumph from Caryl as she yanked it out of his hand and slashed at her torturer. Slashed and slashed and slashed, then whirled and whipped across the face of someone who tried to stop her.

She had to escape then, furious, screaming, throwing everything she could see at those who pursued her. She ran to the road.

Pastor followed. He ran fast, arrowing after the child, frightening her into even greater effort to escape him.

When the cars slewed to a stop, brakes screaming, and

the men piled out, Caryl ran to them. As one of them grabbed her, so did Pastor.

One of the gang members shot him.

The man holding Caryl threw her into the wagon. The other men piled in, and the cars took off, flinging gravel into the faces of the Followers who would have prevented their leaving.

At that instant, Carson—the Logran woman had said their strongest empath knew he was strong enough—controlled his sister over the miles between them. Caryl resisted, but to no avail. Carson let Doc dose her, not as much as the man would have, had Carson not intervened, but enough to put her out for several hours.

With Caryl unconscious, Carson could only assume that the men would drive back to the ghost town. He waited, and while he waited, he thought.

Pastor was dead. Carson had felt Caryl's furious disappointment when the bullet entered the man's heart. She had planned to kill him herself! Her even greater fury at being drugged had passed instantly. Carson felt no pity for his sister. If possible, he hated her more deeply than he ever had admitted to himself he could hate.

His terrible objectivity gave him the reason. He hated *himself* for not finding a way, any way, of getting Caryl out of Rightway before she drowned in the evil they immersed her in by believing—and teaching her—that her natural, normal talents were Satanic possession.

In the hour or more it took the cars to return to the valley, Carson had nothing to do but think.

This situation was entirely his responsibility. It would not have happened it he hadn't tried to free both Mother and himself from the burden of Caryl's abilities and behaviors by taking his sister away. He did not fault himself for the attempt, but for the method he had chosen. Carson had learned too much from Ed about reality to believe any longer that running away from your problems was a successful method of solving them. "Never run *away*," Ed said. "If you've gotta run, always run *to*. An' y' better know, real good, what's gonna be there."

He tried to reject the message of the woman on the radio, but everything she had said was true. She knew things she could know only through psi functions. One thing she'd said pierced his rejection: He was a child.

He *was* a child. Pastor's religion said children weren't responsible, which Carson knew wasn't true. But he'd learned chapter and verse of *The Book of The Way,* chapter and verse of the responsibilities adults had for children. While he could not shuck off the responsibility for having made the wrong choice, he could, and must, share it with a drunken mother, who had dumped her responsibilities on him. And he must share it with an absent father, who had let her.

Carson knew he could not go through life forever blaming himself for not feeling, not acting, not choosing differently. He had done the best he could *then*. If *since* and *now* and *later* proved him wrong, he could only accept his failure, learn from the experience, and go on, trying to do better. "Yesterday is valuable only for the things it taught." Ed. "God forgives us our errors and misdeeds. Can we do less? To forgive ourselves is the most difficult, yet the most important challenge He offers us. Admit thine error, vow to do differently, and go on, forgiven by God and self." *The Book of The Way.*

He *must* forgive himself. Otherwise, tomorrow as Ed thought of it, worthwhile because it offered hope, could never come.

To live with himself, he must also forgive his father. Carson was not sure he understood why his father did not accept the fact that Caryl acted as she did when he wasn't there, but he wondered if Dad wasn't like Ed's ma—what he couldn't see and experience, he believed to be lies. Carson was willing to ask for an explanation—and to try to accept the answer.

He made the decision to forgive his father.

Love her as he did, as he always would, Carson did not forgive his mother. His love for her was something quite apart from her reality, and he knew it.

He sensed the presence of the cars, climbed swiftly down the cliff, and ghosted over to the town to resume his former position behind the house where they had the radio. The men arrived, shouting in triumph, carried Caryl into the radio room, and dumped her on a cot.

"Doc'll check her regularly, starting after midnight," the leader explained to the man who'd been left behind. "When she starts coming to, we'll tie her up. As long as she's out, there's no need, and we don't want to take chances on her being damaged."

The men laughed. "Doc, you'd better keep her doped," a voice unfamiliar to Carson said. "She sure is a witch. If she comes to, she'll probably untie herself, and bleeding hearts like that dame on the radio'll never believe she damaged herself."

More laughter.

"Yeah. Well, no problem for now."

Carson listened as their radio operator contacted the Logran Organization. The man refused to give the Organization complete information, however, telling the person on the other end of the transmission that final instructions

170

would be given the following morning. The kidnappers were taking no chances that the Logran people would come before Caryl was conscious, lest the Organization consider her harmed.

Carson waited.

The men went back to the other house, broke out the booze, and celebrated themselves into drunken stupors.

Now that the time had come to act, Carson had to force his body to move, his mind to think. "I didn't know being angry took that much out of you," he muttered to himself. He could hardly pick up his pack from inside the window. He had to brace it against the house in order to put it on. When he moved away, he nearly stumbled.

His sudden fear of discovery sent a burst of adrenaline through him. He actually could feel it, and it bothered him badly. *No more of that!* He had little enough energy left. To use it up being scared might doom both himself and Caryl. He had to keep going, one foot in front of the other, planning carefully, but being willing instantly to switch to Plan B—if he could think up a Plan B—or even improvise. For now, he must just ask as little as possible of his tired body, move at a steady pace, and hope for the best.

Carson trusted to luck and the luck, and walked to the mine the easiest way—along the road. Raucous song accompanied him. He hadn't lived a life so sheltered that he'd never heard blasphemy or profanity before, but the words made him feel as if the men were vomiting gaseous filth into the clear night air. His normal reaction—to sing something, loud—being impossible, he concentrated on remembering some of the songs Ed had taught him.

The gang must be thieves as well as kidnappers. And they must have made many trips in and out of the valley.

Stored in the mine entrance were piles of goods Carson would swear were stolen and an armory of weapons and ammunition.

Carson looked around. After he brought Caryl in, he would . . . Mental pictures of exactly where to apply stress might have been as brilliantly illuminated as plans on a drafting table. He nodded and made his way through to another passageway. Around a bend was a small niche, quite unnoticeable, even if one had a flashlight. He dropped the pack there, thinking in a detached way that it looked like one more rock.

He moved along the tunnel and took the first right turn, then leaned against the rock and let his super-sense take over. He stood there a long time, following one possible route after another. At last, he smiled. He'd known Ed would never work a mine with only one exit, and the route to the second exit was lethal—for anyone who didn't have his or Ed's abilities. "We can make it," he breathed. The possibility that they might get free took on greater solidity than hope.

Oddly, the use of his extra ability gave him strength. He found he could move more quickly and observe more awarely as he made his way back to the ghost town.

The opening of the door of the living-shack caught him unprepared. In the second before Doc came out, Carson lay full length. Visual adaptation to the dark took Doc an instant or so, and Carson was so still that the man, expecting nothing, did not note him. Doc wove over to the radio room and went in.

Checking on Caryl, Carson thought. *Second time? Third?* He checked his watch. Probably third. No wonder Doc's gait was so unsteady.

Carson probed out to determine Caryl's condition. She

was still fully under, not even beginning to have her mind back yet. What if he hadn't prevented Doc from dosing her as he'd planned? She'd probably be dead! She was a slender child at the best of times. Her expenditure of power took energy. Without an ounce of fat, muscle tissue would have had to provide the fuel she used to build the church, and then to destroy it and hurl heavy weights like popcorn.

Even so, Carson wasn't sure he could carry her all the way through the mine, even if they rested and ate several times. He prayed she'd be able to manage for herself, at least on the worst parts of the dangerous route to the other exit.

He remained where he was until Doc returned to the other shack, then rose and ran to the radio cabin. Now was the best possible moment, with Doc having just checked Caryl's condition. Nevertheless, he did not go in through the front door. He'd heard the creaking of the steps and the loud protest of the door from fifty yards away. The window through which he'd caught his glimpse of the interior was wedged open as far as it would go, probably to let as much air as possible enter. *During the day, that was a good idea,* Carson thought, *but Caryl must be freezing.* He peered in.

No. They weren't taking chances. She was well covered with at least two blankets. *How thoughtful. One for each of us.*

He climbed in, careful not to touch the stick holding the window open, and Indian-footed over to the cot. For now, he'd make a papoose of Caryl in both blankets. That way, he could carry them all easily, and the blankets would cushion her a little when he had to let her slide out the window onto the ground.

Despite believing he was prepared for it, Caryl's slight weight frightened Carson. She breathed shallowly, but he could feel the steady, too-slow beat of her heart against his back when he slung her over his shoulder. All he could do was continue as he was going and hope she lived through it.

Out the window, first Caryl in a bony heap, then Carson, who had some difficulty not stepping on her. He hoisted her up in a fireman's carry and moved around to the rear of the building. He'd take the back way as far as the houses went, then check before they moved into the open. If only all the men stayed inside.

Well, trouble takes care of itself. No point in worrying about it, he quoted Ed.

Carson, a typical Welshman in build, with strong bones and muscles, carried his sister easily. He checked at the corner, decided now was as good as any time, and ran to the mine entrance. No one shouted or shot flashlight beams or bullets after him, and he breathed easily for the first time in fifteen minutes. Would Doc check Caryl on the schedule he'd set up? He doubted it. The unsteadiness of the man's gait indicated that his idea of "regularly" might be off.

Carson sensed out, following his pattern to the other exit, a way that no one but he or Ed could follow without becoming trapped—if not killed outright. When he found a small area where Caryl could remain while he went back to the mine entrance, he set her down.

He knew from his own experience with the drug that Caryl was now mentally aware although physically incapacitated. He had too much to do to put up with Caryl in the state she'd be when she could speak.

"Caryl, I've been there, so I know you can hear me. I've

174

carried you into the mine. You're far enough in that they can't get to you. I'm going back for my pack. We'll need the food, and we may need the water." He pulled off his watch and set it where she could see it. "I'll be back in about an hour. If I don't come—if they catch me—wait until the drug wears off. Stay right here. No matter what, wait. Ed can find you if I . . . if anything happens to me."

20

Nothing happened to him.

He stood in the darkness and shook with reaction from how close he'd cut it. The men, flashlights in hands, guns and rifles at the ready, were within sight from the entrance, coming toward it with what they probably believed was utter silence. He'd had far less time than he'd have liked, but he managed to kick, shove, and manhandle the right rocks. The whole forepart of the cavelike room shook, rumbled, and with the deceptive slowness Carson knew came from his own speeded-up senses, descended. He fled, to wait behind a solid pillar until he got his breath back and time returned to normal, while the whole entry-gang filled with rock. He could not even hear voices, so solid and thick was the plug.

He wondered what the criminals would do now. Get into the cars and make for somewhere else? Probably. At any rate, he had stopped them from using the arsenal—and from getting at all the things they'd stolen. If the authorities were interested, they could bring modern machines into the valley, clear away the rubble, and find it all.

Caryl had recovered from the drug-paralysis by the time he returned with his pack. She clung to him, shaking, and whispered, "You're alive, you're alive. Oh, Carson, I'm so glad you're alive!"

He held her and patted her back. When she was calmer, they ate a little and drank less. Carson opened his pack, located some clothing, and handed it to her. "Here," he said. "Get into these. They'll be too big, but at least they'll be warmer while we work our way through the mine."

"Where are we going?"

"To another exit from the mine. Ed will find us."

"Ed?" Caryl asked. "The old prospector? But I thought he took you away for the—the men."

"I'll explain later," Carson said. "For now, he's a friend. The best friend I've ever had. He'll be there, and he'll help us."

"All right, Carson," Caryl said. "I can wait."

He stared at her in the darkness, unable to see her, but aware of her presence and her attitude. Completely at a loss to explain the latter, he led the way into the perilous darkness.

Carson had been awake for so many hours—and in them had expended so much energy in both action and emotion—that he could not continue far.

"I've got to get some sleep," he admitted finally. "I know it's hard for you in the dark, but there's no other way. If I don't rest, I can't find the way."

"It's OK, Carson," Caryl said, astonishing him again. "I keep my eyes shut. That way, I can't see the darkness. I'm tired, too, though I know I slept—well, sort of—for a long time. Maybe I can go to sleep, too. Can I . . . would you mind holding on to me?"

"Spread out my sleeping bag. We can use the blankets."

With Caryl curled up against him, Carson slept almost instantly.

When he woke, considerably refreshed, they went on. How Caryl stood the trip, Carson could not imagine. He knew what a trip through the dark had meant to Dad. But she kept up, rarely needing help, through all but the most difficult places. He wondered if she was receiving his mind pictures again, hoped it was so, and did not inquire. If she was, and he asked her about it, she might stop. He did not dare to take the chance. During the easiest parts of the trip, he told her about Ed, about living in the cabin, learning about the desert, planning how to help her without taking the chance of involving himself again with Rightway. He expected her to begin railing at him, but she remained silent, holding his hand or his belt as directed, and made few comments.

Caryl smelled the fresh air as soon as he did. "Carson!" she whispered. "Are we there? Can I open my eyes?"

"Not yet," he answered. "I'll tell you when. It's probably not as close as we'd like it to be, but at least we know it's there."

Caryl began to sob, very softly, in what Carson knew to be relief. Greater relief than his, even, because he *knew,* and she had only her trust in him and her fear of what lay behind.

When he led the way out into the star-shine of what must be the next night, he made sure they were well away from the entrance, so she could see the stars and feel the openness, before he said, "When."

"Oh, Carson!" she breathed. "Oh, Carson, we made it! We made it. I knew we would, but I was so scared."

She turned around and burrowed her head into his chest, hugging him so hard that he could scarcely breathe. He looked down at the top of her head, absolutely incredulous.

Before he could think better of it, he said, "You're the bravest person I know, Caryl, and I'm very proud to be your brother."

She hugged him harder, shaking and gasping with her tearless crying. He hoped it was only the reaction of relief, but something about the way she held him, the way he felt about her, told him it was more, it was different. He asked her, but she just shook her head. As if by saying something nice he had taken away her ability to speak, she remained silent.

They were terribly hungry by the time Ed and Stubborn showed up.

Carson took one look at Ed, curled into a ball, and went to sleep. He slept and slept and slept and slept. If hunger hadn't wakened him, he might have died and never known it.

He woke in Ed's cabin. Stubborn had borne him a third time, though Carson did not remember the trip at all. He staggered out of Ed's bed, practically fell, grabbed a chair, and dragged himself to the table. Ed had put a covered plate of corn pone, three cans, and a can opener there. Ham, stewed tomatoes, and peaches. He liked all of them, but had they been brussels sprouts and oysters, both of which he loathed, he would hardly have noticed. Carson ate half the small ham and all of everything else. He staggered back to bed. He got up later and ate again. By evening, he managed to stay awake.

"How did you manage it?" he asked Ed.

Ed glanced back through the doorway toward where Caryl lay, utterly quiet, on the sleeping bags. She had not responded when Carson spoke to her, and Carson worried. Ed's expression indicated equal concern.

Ed's voice was just a little louder than necessary—loud enough that Caryl could hear, too.

"Stubborn 'n' me, we took our us'al route down to Rightway," Ed began, and Carson could hear the storyteller. "So we come inta th' place about our us'al time. Fer th' first time, we was met t'other sidea th' valley. A kid took off arunnin' fer Pastor, an' Betty—y' remember th' woman who's gonna have her baby soon?—she walkt in with us, slow-like. I was real su'prized t' see how far along th' church buildin' was. Betty, she didn't wanna talk much about it. Matter a fact, she didn't wanna talk much atall. So, bein' a good guest, I jest walkt along."

Pastor had come out of the Common House to meet Ed. He was less welcoming than usual, but he did invite the old man to have noon meal. Ed asked about "th' little gal," and was told she was asleep. She was not doing well in the heat and often fell asleep in the middle of the day. She'd have her meal when she woke. Ed expressed sorrow about the boy, not that he felt guilty, but the kid'd died, sure. Pastor said it was God's will because Carson had not been receptive to The Way. They had held a Farewell Ceremony, and the boy's soul was now in God's hands. They would persevere in their duty to the girl. Ed tried to turn the conversation to the construction of the new church, but Pastor found a reason to excuse himself, and no one else would discuss it.

When Pastor returned, the surprisingly silent meal was over. He sent someone for Ed's ore from the safe, helped pack up, and sent him on his way.

Ed arrived at the station in time to set the signals the next morning. On the train, everyone talked about nothing but the Organization's broadcasts. Ed listened. He decided not to visit the sheriff.

He had to go to the assay office, to the bank, and to buy supplies. He did so quickly, intending to take the evening train back, but Jase had run into him. Ed couldn't leave without spending the night, or Jase would have become suspicious. He pretended total ignorance of the matter that had everyone buzzing.

All the way back to Rightway Station the next day, Ed cussed at himself for a stupid old codger. He'd figured out where the men had gone. They had stayed in the area, and somehow, one of them must have followed him when he went over to the new mine.

He hadn't come back to the cabin. Were Carson there— Ed didn't think he would be—he was safe enough. Caryl was the one in danger. Those men had a radio, so would have learned about the reward—and would head for Rightway to assure themselves of Caryl, anyway. Ed went directly to the mine valley. He'd slept only when Stubborn refused to take another step.

When he got to the top of the old road, he heard the cars coming. He found a place to hide Stubborn and himself, lay low while the cars passed, then located a vantage point. He saw Carson. He watched the whole incident. After Carson carried his sister into the mine, Ed went down and removed the distributors from both vehicles. He climbed back up, and he and Stubborn set off for the other exit from the mine. Carson knew the rest.

Distributors! Carson thought.

He had been a Follower too long. Much, much too long.

Ed glanced toward the interior of the cabin. Carson looked in, too. Caryl had turned her back to the door. Was she asleep? He used to be able to tell. Could he now? Despite his sense of having been bludgeoned to pulp, he was still aware of Caryl.

He whispered, "She's asleep."

"I learned somethin' else, too," Ed added, but so softly Caryl could not have heard, even had she been awake.

Carson froze.

"Seems like there's a Missing Persons report out on a couple a' kids named Carson and Caryl Bleeker. Their dad wants 'em back."

Carson sighed. It had to come out sometime. Now was as good as any. The only good thing about telling it was that Ed would listen all the way through, not interrupting or judging, just paying attention. He told Ed.

The old man nodded. "We'll get y' t' a phone that works. Y' kin call yer da' an' set up a place t' meet."

"What about the fake sheriff and his gang?"

Ed smiled. "I did tell Jase about 'em," he admitted. "Had t' think fast t' leave you kids outa it, but I was always a quick thinker. I tol' 'im I'd seed some suspicious types aroun' here, but I didn' tell 'im exactly where he could find 'em 'cause I figgered they mighta took Caryl by then, an' I didn' think we'd want any outsiders to know 'bout her—'an you—with all them rewards bein' offered.

"He tol' me some gang's been causin' trouble hereabouts. We put two 'n' two t'gether and come up with Jase havin' th' gov'ner call out the Guard so's he'd have plenty a backup an' th' element a su'prise. I knowed he'd need more 'n just his deputies. I trust Jase, but I didn' know iffen I could trust whoever he called fer help."

182

Carson nodded. That should take care of the gang. But what if one of them told about Caryl? They wouldn't. One of them had killed Pastor. But the National Guard was also being used by the Logran Organization to search for him and Caryl. That made him nervous.

"Do you think the Organization was able to trace the first radio message?" Carson asked.

"When Stubborn 'n' me was on our way t' you 'n' yer sister, a little copter buzzed over, high 'n' fast, dipped inta th' valley, an' took off. Them low-lifes shot at it, but I don' s'poze bein' hung over helpt their accuracy none. It'd just got away when th' Guard copters come in. I figger th' Organization, then Jase. I knowed he'd find 'em iffen he knowed their gen'ral location. I don't think y' need t' worry about them murderers an' kidnappers no more," Ed finished.

Carson nodded. Yes, when the kidnappers called the Organization, sophisticated instrumentation would have homed in on the location of the transceiver. Someone at the Organization put that together with whatever psionic signals they were getting. Unfortunately, although they knew Caryl wasn't in the valley, they also knew she wasn't under that huge rockfall he'd caused, that they both were alive and somewhere in this area. Would the Organization go to Rightway? Of course. Where else could he and Caryl have been? Then they'd know. They'd find out about Pastor's murder and inform the authorities. Something good would come out of this.

One worry off his shoulders did little to lighten Carson's load of troubles, but it did mean they could start to a phone without looking over their shoulders every fifth step to watch for pursuers. They'd have to listen hard and search overhead for the Organization's helicopter, and possibly keep an eye out for the Guard copters, too. Same thing.

He hoped Ed could figure out some way to hide or disguise them.

"How long will it take?" Carson asked.

"Don' wanna go th' direction they think y'll take—t' th' railroad. An' we ain't goin' west t' where yer da is, neither. We're goin' northeast, inta th' mountains. They won' figger that—nobody's s'pozta've gone through 'em on foot. Mapped from th' air, I hear. I figger I'm th' only one left who knows th' way, an' I don' talk much about what I know. Anybody'd think twice about sendin' them expensive flyin' whirligigs inta th' range. Dangerous winds, narrow gulches, all sortsa problems they won' want." He actually giggled, a high, old man whinny. "One thing none a them people know about. Me!"

Carson gaped. Of course! Ed was the unknown quantity in all of the Organization's planning. They might escape after all!

"Nope, they'll try all th' other places first, an' we'll be long gone."

Ed pulled out an old map and leaned over it. "Yep. Porreyville's practically forgot. An' it's on a county road, so yer da kin git to ya. Think that'll do it.

"Five, six days. Have t' go by th' roundabout way, t' find good water. Can't carry enough fer three people an' a mule."

He had five, maybe six, more days of freedom if all went well. Carson tried to be grateful.

21

They set off the following morning before daybreak. They heard no engines, nor did they see any aircraft other than the very high commercial jets. Ed had some difficulty at times picking up landmarks, and they hiked slowly through country no one might ever have seen, much less traveled.

Carson kept silent, knowing Ed concentrated hard. He was glad, when Ed made comments, that the man had dropped the old prospector. That person was a pose, not Ed's reality, and the return of the Welsh sound somehow heartened Carson.

Caryl sat on a blanket atop Stubborn's pack saddle. She adapted to riding so easily that she might have done it daily since infancy. She obeyed when given an order, but otherwise did not pay attention to either Carson or Ed. Carson worried about his sister. Caryl silent was Caryl sick. He put up with it for three days. On the fourth day, going along a sort of valley between two hills, Stubborn trotted forward as if he knew where he was headed. Ed let the mule lead and waited until Carson caught up with him.

"No place else to go," he explained.

Carson's worry was no longer bearable. He gestured for Ed to drop well back with him and voiced his concern. "She was . . . well, she acted just like a normal person from the time she recovered from the dope until we got out of the mine. Then I told her I thought she was the bravest person I'd ever known, and I was proud to be her brother. She hasn't said a word since."

Ed shook his head, sighed, and continued along the valley without saying anything for several minutes. When he did speak, his words were not a direct answer.

"In her whole life, from what you tell me, your sister has never had to pay the piper but has always danced at her pleasure—unless you kept her from it. When you stopped her, she had no way to learn why she should not."

"If I hadn't," he explained, "she'd really have hurt people, even killed them."

"When she was a baby, before she had much strength or particular targets, she would have hurt no one. If she had not been allowed to escape the consequences of her actions, it is likely she would have stopped."

"But it scared Mother," Carson protested. "She cried and shook, and she dropped Caryl a couple of times. Once, when I was about five, Mother stayed in bed all day. She didn't feed Caryl or me, but I was old enough to find food for myself. Caryl screamed all day long. I couldn't stand it. I didn't know what to do. Mother just put a pillow over her head and cried, too. Whenever I'd go into Caryl's room, she'd try to hurt me. I finally got a bottle of formula out of the refrigerator, warmed it in the microwave, and gave it to her. I couldn't get her to stop crying any other way."

"And established the pattern you have followed ever since," Ed said. He sighed. "You were too young to have such a responsibility—and no way of knowing what you had done. It would not have killed Caryl to starve for a day, but you had no way of knowing that. Yes, it was the only thing you could do."

After a long pause, Ed went on. "Had you yet discovered you could stop her from moving things?"

"No," Carson replied. "I found that out the next September. Mother didn't let me go to kindergarten because she had to have help with Caryl. When I turned six, she had to let me go to school. I wanted to—anywhere to get out of the house when Dad wasn't there. Mother was sick for a week before school started. I didn't see how I could go. The first day of school I went in and told Caryl that she wasn't to move anything with her mind all day long. I was mad, really tearing-things-up mad. I ran out of the house and all the way to school."

Ed's involved listening was as good as a conversation.

Carson went on. "School was great. I loved it. Mother taught me to read when I was about three-and-a-half, and Dad taught me arithmetic and a lot of algebra and geometry, so I was ahead of most of the kids and could just have fun. When I had to go home, I didn't want to. I hid in the bushes until I got so hungry I had to go in."

"Caryl had been good all day, and Mother had fed and taken care of her."

"So, from then on, you were the control. Caryl never learned how to behave like a normal child, never got beyond the earliest baby stage of 'Me. Only me.' "

Carson nodded.

"She is nine, you say?"

"Ten, now."

"Ten years before she discovered that the other people in the world do not exist solely for the purpose of serving her. Ten years of not knowing that all of them are as important to themselves as she is to herself. Ten years until she found out that if she controls people by using her talents, they will destroy her. I think she does not speak because, in some way, your words made her remember her life in Rightway. I believe she is in shock."

"I wonder what happened," Carson said.

"Whatever it was, she earned it," Ed said, "and richly deserved worse, I'll be bound."

"No," Caryl said. The single syllable was so soft that only Stubborn heard. He flicked his ears. "No," Caryl said louder.

Carson looked at Ed. The two walked briskly to catch up, then kept pace with Stubborn, one on either side.

"I don't know how you could be proud to be my brother," Caryl whispered. "I've been the worst sister in the whole world!"

Carson didn't know what to say.

"Nobody should be a slave," Caryl went on. "You told me that, Carson. You said I made you a slave, so you had the right to free yourself. I didn't know what you meant. I thought *I* was *your* slave. Lots of times you kept me from doing what I wanted to do. I thought I had the right to pay you back. I understand, now."

"Just what do you understand, Caryl?" Ed asked.

"What being a slave is like," she answered. "Pastor taught me. With that whip thing. I said and did what he wanted me to, or he whipped me."

Carson was angry. Angry at Pastor, true, who deserved

his anger. Angry at himself. Who had kept Caryl from suffering the just consequences of her actions? He had.

Caryl was crying, tearless as always, but making the soft sounds Carson knew to accompany her deepest misery. He didn't know quite what to do. She wasn't trying to force him into doing anything, and he had nothing to fight against. He patted her. She took his hand tentatively, then clung so hard that her grip hurt.

"Oh, Carson! I wanted you so much. Nothing like that ever happened to me when you were there. I wanted you to take care of me!"

Carson started to say that he would, that he hurt as much for her as she herself hurt.

Ed's voice intervened. "Carson will help you the way any good brother would help his little sister. He will never stand between you and the consequences of the way you use your talents. Never again will he—how did you put it, lad?—'Say, "No!" and mean it.' He will warn you, explain why you shouldn't, suggest other things you might do. If you decide to do it anyway, he will let you. Only if you are going to harm someone or destroy something important will he stop you. Then he will use the paralysis. If you have to learn by pain, you will have to hurt."

"That's what Pastor said," Caryl wailed.

Ed did not react. "Why did he do this?" he asked.

"Because I wouldn't do what he wanted any other way!" Caryl answered.

"That is the life of a slave," Ed agreed.

Caryl sniffed for several minutes. They let her.

When she seemed a bit calmer, Ed continued. "Now, lass, let us examine this matter. Did Carson ever hurt you to make you do what he wanted you to do?"

Caryl started to speak several times, and at last muttered,

"Not until after the earthquake. Before, he'd just keep me from doing things I shouldn't do so I wouldn't get in trouble."

Carson gaped.

"And after the earthquake?"

"He slapped me, but I guess he had to once. I wasn't paying attention. The other time I said a really bad word. From then on. He let me decide what to do mostly, he didn't hurt me," Caryl admitted. "He changed, though. When I tried to do stupid things like striking a match when the gas main was broken, or making a big scene, or showing him how much better I was than he—not letting him have the keys—he paralyzed me. I guess I hurt because I wouldn't give in—even if I knew he was right."

Carson was so stunned that he was dumb.

"Then, were you Carson's slave?"

Caryl shook her head. "No."

"Why did he believe he was your slave? How did you hurt him if he did not do as you told him to do?"

Caryl's voice was a mere thread. "Every time Pastor made me work on the church, I'd remember Mother saying she couldn't take it if I got out of hand. Carson would just have to do something. So he had to be around all the time, never doing what he wanted to do. I remembered how often I acted up just because Carson did want to do something else, something without me. I wouldn't let him. So I treated him the way Pastor treated me, in a way. He couldn't get away from me any more than I could get away from Pastor. That means I was just as bad as Pastor. If I didn't do what Pastor told me, I got whipped. If Carson didn't do what I wanted him to, I acted up, and Mother made Carson do it. I hurt on the outside, but Carson hurt on the inside. I knew it, and I didn't care! I wanted him to hurt."

She was crying again, sobbing so hard that her phrases came out in little bursts, not always quite understandable. "When he told me he was proud to be my brother, I knew he shouldn't be. I was so dreadful! He ought to hate me."

Carson stopped himself before he let his thought out of his mouth. *I did. Most of the time,* wouldn't help any at the moment. Maybe never.

"Did Pastor want you to hurt?" Ed asked.

"I thought he did. I was sure he did. He kept saying he didn't, that if I didn't like the life of a slave, all I had to do was accept The Way, and I'd be doing what I *wanted* to do, not what he *made* me do. I'd be happy to do God's work, as he did, no matter how hard it was. I always thought Carson should want to do what I told him. He never did, so it was all right to hurt him. It wasn't all right. It was all wrong. Nobody should have to *want* to do what somebody else says they *have* to do!"

Carson had trouble believing his ears. This was Caryl?

"That is a true thought," Ed stated. "You might remember it when you have recovered from this experience."

Caryl sat up straighter, sniffed, rubbed her hands across her eyes, and tried to stop crying. "I'm not going to forget it," she said. "All the time Pastor was making me do what he wanted, never what I wanted, I thought about Carson. Did he hate me as much as I hated Pastor? I kept thinking he couldn't. He'd never done anything terrible to me, the kind of thing I wanted to do to Pastor."

"Why do you suppose he didn't?" Ed asked.

Caryl whispered, "I don't know."

"Perhaps you will, one day," Ed said. "But today is not the day. And you may not ask him; it is a thing you must decide for yourself."

Carson stared at the side of Ed's head. Why must Caryl not ask him? *Because I don't know the answer,* he realized.

"Now that you know you do not want to be the master, one who hurts people and makes them hate her, now that you know you do not want to be a slave, one who is hurt—and hates—how can you keep from being either a master or a slave?"

Caryl turned to Ed. Carson could not see her face. "Oh, Ed," she said. "I don't *know* how! I used to try not to act that way sometimes, but I got mad . . . and things happened."

"Things happened?"

"I made things happen." She whispered her admission. "Afterward, I'd wish I hadn't done it, but I knew I'd do the same thing the next time, so I always tried to believe I was right."

"*Always* is a great deal longer than you have lived," Ed said. "It comes to me that you have made the first step toward changing. You do not yet use the words, but one day you will be able to say that you were sorry and ashamed. To feel that way does not mean you must tell yourself you were right. Perhaps you could decide not to do it again."

"I have! Thousands of times. It never works. What am I going to *do* with it?" she burst out. "The power? It builds up and builds up, and I can't hold on to it, and it makes me think horrible things—like wanting to hurt and kill people—and it gets away from me!"

"That is a thing to think on," Ed said slowly. "Answers to difficult questions do not come easily."

Carson stared at Caryl's shuddering back. What would it be like if he couldn't use the luck, if it didn't automatically switch on to help him catch balls and deflect falling objects, to avoid tripping, to know his way in the dark, to do all the things he knew other people couldn't? What would it be like to have it all dam up inside? He found himself shaking as hard as Caryl.

Ed reached a hand over Stubborn's rump and grasped Carson's shoulder. Carson felt comforted.

Ed continued to follow Stubborn until they came to a break in the hills to the east. He pulled the lead rope to halt the mule. He examined their surroundings. At last, he sighed and nodded. "We are almost through the mountains. I had planned to go over another pass—one I found many years ago—" He pointed along their line of march and somewhat to the west—"but we must have more time to discuss this." He pointed again, eastward between the rocky hills. "Only four or five miles that way is a spot where we may camp. True, it is known—to few, but to some. At this time of the year, we should be safe enough. We shall go there."

Ed turned Stubborn and led the way. Stubborn picked up his pace slightly. Ed snorted. "Sensible beast. He knows water is closer this way," he explained. "The faster he arrives, the sooner he rests."

Carson was pleased. Maybe he would have an extra day. He had even filled the miles of silent hiking with daydreams of locating a place he could find water, build a cabin, and live, sending Caryl on with Ed. He couldn't. He knew it. But what lay at the end of this journey was something he did not want to experience. Not only his father's anger and disappointment. Those, he felt he could counter with his own. Facing his father, whom he knew he must have worried almost out of his mind, would be so difficult that he did not know how he could manage it.

When they reached Ed's destination, a tiny canyon filled with coolness and green, Carson was surprised and delighted. One of the rare, lovely, desert springs welled up and poured its waters along a bed before they soaked in and disappeared. Stubborn stopped with his nose in the stream and waited to be unpacked.

"Let us begin," Ed said as if continuing the conversation he had left in silence two hours before, "by asking if you have some power now?"

Caryl nodded. "Not a lot. Some."

"How could you choose to use it to be helpful?"

A tentative, unpracticed smile tried to force its way through the dirt and sweat-streaks on Caryl's face. "I could unpack," she ventured.

"A good way," Ed decreed. "Carson will locate something burnable and make a fire. I will feed and groom Stubborn. You will unpack. We will do our jobs with our bodies. You will sit over there on that clump of grass and use your mind only."

"Yes, Master," Caryl said.

"Yes, Ed!" Carson corrected. "He is your teacher, not your master. You are a student, not a slave. If you disagree with what he says, you can say so."

Caryl bit her lip. "Yes, Ed," she whispered.

"But if you do not do your fair share of the work," Ed said, "or if you try to use your power in some way I do not agree you should, I will ask Carson to prevent you."

Caryl looked at each of them. "I'm trying to remember, even if I don't want to. I'm trying not to get mad."

"Put that energy into unpacking," Ed suggested.

Caryl breathed hard, then relaxed. "Please help me down." She held out her arms to Ed. "I really need it. I don't think my legs will hold me up. They hurt when I try to move."

Ed's eyes twinkled. He lifted Caryl free of the packs, swung her off, and carried her to the grass. "Too wet," he decided. He held her over a flat rock.

"You might see to the comfort of your poor, bruised tailbone by padding your seat with a blanket or two," he advised.

194

Caryl giggled, actually giggled!

Carson could feel the beginning of her power-wiggle. He controlled himself.

The straps holding Stubborn's pack saddle unknotted themselves. The packs rose, then settled neatly onto dry ground near Caryl's rock. The blanket she had used as a saddle unfolded, flapped briskly, refolded itself, and plopped down on the rock.

Ed set her down gently. She gasped, and Carson could see-feel the pain. Caryl said nothing, just took a deep breath and clenched her fists.

"Yell. It's a healthy way to express yourself," Ed said.

Caryl shook her head. "It's better now. But could I lie on my front instead of sitting on my poor, bruised tailbone, oh, teacher?"

Ed and Carson both chuckled.

Caryl's unused, squeaky giggle joined their amusement. She had actually made a very small joke on herself!

Ed nodded portentously. "A good suggestion, student. Do that thing."

Caryl flopped forward, rearranged her blanket, and wiggled over onto it. She sighed. "Better. Lots better." She looked around, almost as if she did not want to look directly at Ed or Carson. Her eyelids lowered.

When she raised them, she looked up into Carson's eyes. She said, loudly enough that he heard her easily, "Thank you, Carson."

Carson was so surprised—and so glad—that laughter was the only appropriate response. He could laugh, for she knew how good he felt and that he wouldn't be laughing at her, but Ed might not understand. Carson snorted instead, winked at Caryl, and said, "And?"

Caryl flirted her eyelashes down and glanced at him with

something of her old cute expression. She looked up at Ed. "Thank you, Ed," she said sweetly.

Carson needn't have worried about Ed's understanding. As he and Caryl burst into uncontrollable chortles of relief and pleasure, Ed *ho ho ho*'d like a disguised Welsh Santa Claus. He pulled Caryl's unkempt ponytail gently and patted Carson's back so hard that the boy ran forward four steps, still laughing.

"On with the chores," Ed said.

22

"Hi! What's so funny?" called a voice.

In the instant it took Carson to locate the speaker, enough thoughts passed through his mind to have taken him an hour at any other time. Who was she? Why was she here? Could she have anything to do with the Logran Organization or with anyone who was searching for him and Caryl? Was she out to earn the reward money? Could she have seen Caryl mind-moving the packs and the blanket? . . . These were only the tip of the iceberg.

He saw four young people. The girl who spoke wasn't a lot older than he. One boy was about her age, and the other two were older. They were backpackers, well equipped for the desert. Their appearance was normal for the situation . . . if the situation were any other than the one he was in.

"Hi, y'rselvz," Ed called. "Nothin' much. Jest havin' a little joke on us."

Carson could reassure himself about one thing. They couldn't have seen. The spring rose in a narrow defile between hills. Until one practically fell into the little valley, one couldn't see it, even if he knew where to look—as, undoubtedly, these people did.

"On me, really," Caryl said as the four approached and slung off their packs. "I've never ridden a mule before, and I'm too sore to sit down."

Carson gulped. This was Caryl?

The oldest of the boys stepped forward holding out his hand to Ed. "I'm Paul Oakfield," he said. "My sister, Tallie, Randy Frandsen, Basil King." He indicated first the younger, then the older of the other two boys. "We're on a long-weekend hike."

"Call me Ed," the old man said, shaking the hand. "Everybody else does. Lost m' last name so long ago I'm not sure I remember it. These here 'r' m' gran'kids, Carey an' Sonny. Well, that ain't his name, but I al'uz call 'im that, so he's usta it, even if he don't like it much."

"David," Carson said, playing up. "I'll answer to Sonny for Gramps, but not for anybody else." He hoped he could answer to David. It was his middle name—even if he did spell it Daffyd, as the Welsh did. He also hoped "Carey" could remember to call him by it.

"Can't say I blame you," Randy said. "I don't answer to Randolph either, though I have to admit my parents cursed me with it."

"I hope you don't mind our joining you," Paul said. "This is the only water around, and we didn't expect to find other campers."

Old Ed waved away the concern. "Water's free; we're glad a' th' company. Make y'rselvz t' home."

By the time the seven of them had rolled out bedrolls on the narrow ledges, started a fire—one, for the whole lot of them, in the fire-ring Ed constructed deftly—and settled themselves, the swift, early night of February in the desert had dropped over the hills, filling their tiny cup of green and darkening everything but the stars and the leaping flames. Carson's concern about the identities of the backpackers had tucked itself into a deep recess in his mind as of no particular importance. They were just what they said they were—four teenagers on a hike.

"How come you kids ain't in school?" Ed asked. "You'da thought I was kidnappin' m' gran'kids, th' things that school wanted t' know."

"We are, sort of," Tallie said. She chuckled. "Mother said we'd learn as much out with Paul as we would in any classroom, and oh, was she right. But this is a lot more fun."

"My birthday present," Basil said. "I'm not as old as I look. Sixteen today."

"Happy birthday," Ed, Carson, and Caryl said.

"I invite you to join in my birthday dinner." Basil pulled a huge can out of his pack.

A whole ten-pound canned turkey! Carson cheered.

"My birthday is not my birthday without turkey," Basil said. "I tried to find a smaller can—say, three pounds—but they were all out. I wouldn't have carried it all this way if we were going to be out longer—but I figured I could manage it with a light pack."

"I've got two cans of candied yams," Tallie said, producing them. "And marshmallows."

Paul had cans of green beans and mushrooms and tiny white onions. He poured them all into one pot.

Randy added the final touch. Cherry pie filling and a package of piecrust! "Basil does not like cake," he informed the three surprised people. "I also have a can of icing and candles."

"Icing on cherry pie?" Caryl sounded incredulous.

"To each his own," Basil replied, straight-faced. "You may scrape the icing off, if you wish."

Caryl shook her head. "I think it sounds good. Sort of like warm ice cream."

"Not a bad description," Randy agreed. He set to work efficiently and soon had a pie baking in a fold-up oven. The smells were ambrosial.

"We didn't come s' well prepared," Ed said, "but I kinda think stewed tomatoes'd go good."

"Um," Tallie said. "I love stewed tomatoes."

"We've got peaches, too," Caryl contributed.

"Got your handy-dandy box of spices?" Basil asked Randy.

"Do I ever go camping without them?"

Randy took the big can of peaches out of Caryl's hand. "Spiced peaches, here we come."

Ed made coffee; Tallie made tea; Caryl opened a can of milk without being told.

Probably, Carson thought later, as he lay by the fire on his sleeping bag, *it's the food.* He felt great, full and comfortable, and more at ease than he'd felt in so long that he hardly recognized the sensation.

It was more than that, a lot more. He liked these four strangers. They were so easy with each other, so genuinely friendly. They teased a little now and then, but no one said anything cutting. They were interested in everything. Paul could have taught a course in astronomy and celestial navigation, Carson felt sure. Basil took out a guidebook, a flashlight, and a pouch full of snippets of this and that, and proceeded to classify and file each of the pieces of vegetation. The others looked and listened and asked intelligent questions. Obviously, Basil was interested in healing. All the specimens were those the Indians had used for medicines. Ed contributed a good deal to that discussion and suggested other plants Basil should watch for. Randy's collecting sack held various edible things that grew in the desert. Thanks to Ed, Carson could join in that conversation, and they welcomed his contributions.

Caryl, who said little but watched and listened avidly, was more pleasant than Carson had ever known her. She invariably called him David—and as naturally as if she always had. Whatever there was about these four people, it had a positive influence on Caryl, Carson thought. He wished he could get to know them better, have them for friends. He liked them.

When the moon rose, silver-bright in the dark, starry sky, Tallie turned to watch. They all did. A period of still peace held for a long, long minute.

" 'Shine on, shine on harvest moon,' " Caryl began.

Well, it wasn't harvesttime, Carson thought, but the moon was beautiful.

All the Bleekers had good voices, and Caryl's clear soprano, surprisingly mature for her age, blended into the moonlight and the silence without breaking either. " 'Up in the sky,' " Tallie joined in. Her voice was fine, but Carson could tell she was singing a part she usually didn't— the alto. While the notes were right, he could hear just a hint of hesitation.

" 'I ain't had no lovin' since . . .' "

All three of the boys sang well, too. Randy, softly, on the tenor, obviously taking care not to strain and break. Paul's baritone was full, strong, but restrained, so as to keep the balance. To Carson's surprise, Basil sang alto with Tallie. *He really is sixteen and still can use his boy-voice,* Carson thought. *No, that's not right. It's like the trained male altos in the church choir. Bet he's a bass when he uses his man-voice. Wonder why he isn't singing that?*

Old Ed added the bass. Carson swallowed sudden tears.

Well, if somebody as big and as mature as Basil could sing alto, Carson could, too, without anybody thinking it sissy. That'd mean Tallie could go up with Caryl, on the soprano, where she belonged. He joined in. Tallie caught on instantly. They sang it again, and the blend was perfect.

" 'In the evening, by the moonlight,' " Tallie started the next one.

They sang for hours, never loudly, never carelessly. From one old favorite to another. Carson had never been so happy.

When the fire died to rose-hearted ashes, Caryl was more than half asleep, and sleep seemed, somehow, the right next event.

" 'All through the Night,' for happy dreams," Tallie whispered.

When the last note faded, no one spoke. Something very special had happened, and words might have spoiled it.

All my life, Carson thought, *I'll remember tonight.* He put tonight into his memory, into the special place he could go when things got too tough to bear. A number of good things were there—Ed, every minute with Ed—and the days and nights alone on the desert—and that moment of peace when he thought he'd lost Caryl, though he was a little ashamed of that, now—and the few times he'd had with his father, alone. Singing. Da sang. Like Ed. A true Welsh bass. Maybe he'd be a bass, some day. Carson slept.

Morning came later than usual. They'd stayed awake far

too late last night for the sun to waken them at daybreak. Tallie took Caryl with her when she went off for some privacy. She came back without her.

"Basil, what have you got for awful saddle sores?" she asked her friend's somnolent form.

He didn't answer, so she nudged him gently with a foot.

He groaned, but sat up and pulled his pack over so he could rummage in it. "Try this," he said, handing up a tube. "At least it'll stop infection and anesthetize the area. Hold on. I'll give you some sterile pads and tape.

"Why don't you suggest she use her sleeping bag instead of a blanket if she's going to sit atop Stubborn's packs?" he asked. "Should be better padding."

Something about that question bothered Carson enough to waken him fully. Had Caryl told about using a blanket that way? He couldn't remember, but he thought she hadn't.

Oh, for Pete's sake, he thought, disgusted. *She must've.*

Unfortunately, he was awake, so he decided he'd get up. Ed was not in his blanket roll, so it was time for the third of their party to rouse himself.

They prepared a breakfast of leftover turkey and gravy poured over Ed's succulent skillet bread, the preparation of which Randy watched as if he were a student in a Cordon Bleu Cooking School and Ed were the Master Chef. Randy being interested in cooking struck Carson as odd, but . . . *Why not?*

Because Randy didn't strike him as a future chef, that's why.

Carson couldn't assign the terms "unnatural" or "forced" to Randy's interest; it just seemed . . . as if Randy had another interest more important to him.

Just like me, Carson thought. *Like the way I feel about big machines. There aren't any, so I pick up anything else.*

He hardly noticed stumping off into the wilderness to relieve himself; he was too busy thinking. He'd learned a lot at the commune, though he'd resented every second of it. He knew how to care for a half dozen kinds of animals. He knew how to cultivate and harvest vegetable and grain crops. He'd learned at least fifty new songs—principally hymns, of course, but most of them joyous and robust. He'd learned to dance reels and squares and contras, and so many play-party games he'd not stopped to count. He could scrub and disinfect a privy—and clean a room of any size—efficiently and quickly. He could prepare vegetables and meats (few of those, though the Followers did not disdain any food God put on earth for the sustenance of His people) and even cook simple meals for large numbers of people. He could candle an egg. He'd helped construct three windmills. He could—well, he *might* be able to dress a grinding stone. He'd watched Benaiah dress the stones of the wind-driven mill. He knew how simple milling was done. He was sure he could handle a drill-rig, though he'd only watched. He wandered back to the campsite still revealing to himself how much his months with the Followers had taught him.

"What's with you?" Tallie asked him.

He shook his head, looked at her as if he'd never seen a human face before, and answered slowly, "I'm not sure. I guess, well . . ."

Ed called, "Sonny," before Carson could finish his sentence.

In that double syllable, Carson caught warning. He went cold. *Good Pete!* He'd been about to tell Tallie who he was, where he'd been, what he'd learned!

"Yes, Gramps," he said. He almost ran over to Ed.

"Yer breakfast's gettin' cold," Ed said.

The backpackers were packed up and ready to go before Carson, Ed, and Caryl were. The four bade their companions-of-a-night a good journey and hiked out of the valley.

Carson watched them go with a sensation of terrible loss. He'd never see them again, and they were the only four people on earth, barring his father and Ed, he truly felt were his friends.

Tallie, last up the slope, turned and waved. "See you," she called.

Carson, waving to her, wished he could believe he would.

"See you," Caryl called back.

23

Two days later, six days from Ed's cabin, the three of them and Stubborn ambled into the little town of Porreyville.

The six days had been the happiest of Carson's life. He recognized this to be truth, an unbelievable reality he did not choose to delve into deeply. Caryl had not once, not *once,* pulled any of the previous behaviors Carson had believed unchangeable. Together, the three of them had worked out ways in which Caryl could use her powers both safely and helpfully—and to have fun, as well. She improved the rocky trail considerably, walled a high, narrow stretch that gave her the heebie-jeebies, cleaned up a messy campsite, and did all their packing and unpacking. She also tried silly things like bouncing rocks and making platoons of pebbles perform complicated aerobatics. In sheer good spirits, she braided Ed's hair (and beard), zipped Carson's jacket open and closed, and tried all sorts of innocent manipulations. Carson had almost as much fun watching as she did performing.

Ed wouldn't let them sing during the day. "Too much dust. Bad for the throat." But they sang around their campfire each evening. Ed taught Carson and Caryl enough Welsh to learn the words to some lovely songs. "All through the Night" was the first.

Porreyville was one street wide, three streets long. Carson had never seen anyplace like it, hadn't known such towns existed, certainly not in this part of the country. They might well have been in the nineteenth century except for the modern automobiles. There were few, but Carson noted and classified each one almost without thinking about it. The bus station had a phone. Carson started over to use it.

"Carson," Caryl said.

The sound of her voice alerted him like a Mayday. He stopped.

"I want to talk to Daddy when you're done, please."

Why did that simple request sound sirens and alarm bells in his mind? Because she didn't demand to be first, to be only, didn't assume he'd put in the call and automatically hand her the phone? Because she didn't revert to the Caryl she'd been?

He didn't know, so he nodded. "OK. I'll give you the phone."

Carson didn't want to. With all of his intuition, none of his intellect, screaming, he did not know what to do. In truth, Carson had never realized he intuited. He did not know what to call the way he . . . felt? . . . sensed? . . . thought?

He frowned at Caryl, went to the phone, and called Dad's office number.

"Bleeker Engineering," the operator answered. "Good morning."

"This is Carson Bleeker," Carson said. He heard his own voice as if it were a stranger's. "May I please speak to my father?"

"Carson! Is it really you?"

Carson had met her. What was her name? *Oh, yes.*

"It really is, Marilyn," he said. "I'm OK, and so is Caryl. Is Dad there?"

"Oh, Carson, he's not. Hold on. I'll page him."

"No." Carson didn't want to use up Ed's money on a long wait. "When you get him, have him call . . ." He read the number of the pay phone at least three times before the symbols made any sense. He clenched his teeth and blinked hard, determined to pay attention, then repeated the phone number twice, so he could be sure Marilyn had it correctly. "It's a pay phone. We'll stay here waiting for the call no matter how long it takes."

"Don't go away. Oh, Carson. We're so glad! I'll get him right away!"

Carson hung up the phone and wandered away from the installation.

"Not there?" Ed asked.

"He'll call back," Carson answered automatically.

He concentrated on trying to understand what was wrong. Something was, and he couldn't figure out what. He found a bench and sat on it.

The time between calls probably was no more than ten minutes, but Carson felt as if he had waited ten years—or a hundred—before he heard the ring. He sprang up and raced to the phone.

"Carson?" said Dad's voice.

"Yes, Da," Carson said.

"Thank God."

Neither of them said anything for a minute or so. Carson couldn't think of anything to say, and his father, obviously, was crying.

"Where are you?"

"In a little town in the high desert named Porreyville. It's north and east of Jackson."

"You do know the Logran Organization has every man, boy, and dog in the state out searching for you? You must be careful."

"We know. It's why we're here. So far, I don't think we've been spotted. You'll find out why later."

"Can you stay there safely?"

Carson looked around.

"There doesn't seem to be any place to stay. We can come back, though, whenever you get here."

"Hold on, son. I'll check the map."

Carson held on for several months.

"Found it. I'll be there tomorrow morning about eleven, possibly twelve o'clock. Depends on how far I can get on a plane and how bad the roads are to drive. Where will you be?"

"At the bus station."

"Good."

"Da? Caryl wants to talk to you."

"Put her on."

Carson turned and held out the phone.

"Caryl?"

His sister walked over and took the phone out of his

hand. She spoke into the microphone. "Hello, Daddy. . . . I'm fine. When are you coming? . . . I just want you to know two things. First, I love you very much, and I'm sorry I've been such an awful person. Second, I won't be here when you get here. I'm going to the House of Logran."

Caryl hung up the phone.

Carson felt as if he had been slugged in the solar plexus. He could not breathe. He could not even see properly.

Caryl looked at him with an expression he had never before seen on her face. Pity? Sorrow?

"I'm sorry, Carson," he heard but he did not believe. "I've found out a lot about me, and I'm not a nice person at all. There's a chance I might learn how to be one, if I get where I ought to be. That's at the House of Logran. I told them where to come, and they'll be here for me before you can do anything about it."

How could she tell them? Carson was in panic. Through his absolute horror and desperation, he realized he was hearing the sound of a helicopter. He still could not move.

"I hope you can persuade Daddy to come there, or at least to meet them. They're good people. I know. I'm a telepath. You're not, though you do send pictures. We're both empaths, but you're a thousand times better than I am. I can only tell you to believe what you feel, not what you think. What you think—and what Daddy thinks—about the House of Logran is all wrong."

Caryl walked over to the porch rail where Stubborn was tied. She stroked his nose and patted his neck. "Thank you, Stubborn. I forgive you for every saddle sore."

Ed had returned to stand by the mule, whom the approaching helicopter disturbed. Caryl reached over the railing and hugged the old man.

"I'm sorry, Ed," she said. "You're the nicest person I ever knew. I love you. I hope I see you again."

Carson watched as his little sister walked down the steps. The helicopter dropped into the intersection.

The door opened.

Caryl got in.

The helicopter rose.

After it had risen, turned, and started away, Carson could move.

Ed held his arm, a look of worry behind the bushy beard and eyebrows. "You all right, son?" he asked.

Carson shook him off. "I'm OK." He blurted, almost yelling, "Why didn't you stop her?"

"I missed it," Ed said. "I did not hear what you spoke of, and I thought she was coming down the steps to get back on Stubborn. Until she walked right out to that . . . conveyance of the devil . . . I did not realize what she planned to do."

" 'Conveyance of the devil' is right," Carson growled. "The people in it *are* devils. Didn't you see the 'L' on the copter? That's the logo of the Logran Organization!" Carson's voice rose to a scream. He was completely unaware of the attention his behavior caused.

Ed said something in Welsh that could only have been swearwords.

He switched to English. "The people in it are Paul and Tallie Oakfield."

Carson, caught by every negative emotion, became trapped in stilltime.

Ed led him over to Stubborn, helped him on, and led the mule down the main street to the sheriff's office. When he helped Carson off, he muttered, "Only place y' kin be safe from good citizens who wanna be sure y' git where yer sister's goin'—an' they git th' blood money. Dan's all right. I know 'im. I'll git 'im t' call yer da t' tell 'im where yer at. Y' kin wait here 'til he comes."

Even the fact that Ed was going to leave, did leave, walked away down the narrow street in the too-hot February sunshine without ever looking back, did not penetrate Carson's terrible combination of fear and terror, frustration and rage, self-condemnation for having been so easily taken in by Tallie and Paul—and Randy and Basil. The loss of one of his few good places to go, the only people he'd ever felt were friends was, quite literally, torture. The pain was so bad that he moaned. More than anything, he was overwhelmed by a feeling of total helplessness. He sat on a cot in an unlocked cell and stared at his hands. *What was he going to tell Dad?*

The sheriff, Dan, tried to be kind. Carson didn't know he existed. Dan brought him dinner. Carson didn't know it. When it got late, Dan's night man, a deputy, saw to it that he had another blanket and a pillowcase. Some time during the night, Carson lay down. He did not sleep until almost dawn.

He woke in his father's arms, to the sound of his father's voice.

Carson was inconsolable. He was only thirteen, and he was a total failure. Everything he had done had turned out wrong. He cried, tearless, suffering, for hours—all the way back to the airport in the car, all the way back to the city in the plane, all the way back to the apartment his father had rented near his company's building.

His father called the doctor, persuaded him to drop by the apartment on his way home, then persuaded Carson to take the pills the doctor prescribed. They helped. Carson slept again and woke still drug-isolated from the last months, yet remembering them clearly.

He started at the earthquake and told his father everything—everything he'd done, said, felt, and experienced.

It took nearly twenty hours. Carson could hardly croak. He still wasn't hungry. Mr. Bleeker didn't force. He just handed Carson another pill and a glass of water, then held him until he fell asleep.

When Carson woke again, he felt empty—physically, mentally, and emotionally—but back in command of himself.

His father heard him stir and walked over to the bedside. "Breakfast?" he inquired.

Carson nodded. He sat up. Everything spun, but the dizziness went away in a moment.

Mr. Bleeker smiled reassurance. "Just hunger. You'll be OK when you get some food in you."

Carson turned the ends of his lips upward. "Thanks, Da," he whispered.

Mr. Bleeker understood.

"I love you, Carson," he said. "I think you did very well indeed. You have nothing to blame yourself for or feel guilty about that you haven't already paid for ten times over." His mouth twitched in what he probably meant to be a comforting smile. "You can make nine other errors of judgment, free."

He looked away, swallowed, then went on. "I am the one who has my paying to do, and I have far less excuse than you. None, to be strictly honest. To begin with, how would you like to have a full-time father?"

Carson shook his head. "Won't work, Da, and we both know it. But we could start with a . . . a regular part-time father?"

Mr. Bleeker stared down at his son. "Grew up on me, didn't you? And I wasn't there to know."

If this emptiness was what being grown up felt like, Carson wished he never had. But Da was no more capable of being a full-time father than he was of finding his way out of an abandoned mine. They'd just have to start over, differently.

"I love you, Da," he said.

They hugged each other hard, the conversation over, the new beginning made. Mr. Bleeker picked Carson up and took him out to the kitchen for breakfast.

"I sent the money to Jim," Mr. Bleeker said.

Carson stared at him, confused. The memory of taking Jim's name and address from the car Caryl had damaged took a moment or so to return.

"Thanks, Da," he said.

"Good man, that," his father said. "Wouldn't let me send a cent more than he'd paid to have it repaired." He smiled. "I did, though. Told him to take all the men out for a beer bust, on us. That, I think he'll accept."

Carson smiled back. He thought so, too.

That afternoon, Mr. Bleeker telephoned the House of Logran. Ten minutes later, he had a meeting set up. He refused to come to the House. She refused to come to the city. They agreed to meet halfway in a neutral setting. She suggested one of the semi-permanent Army posts—surely he didn't think the House could influence the whole contingent? He agreed. Tomorrow at ten A.M. She would not bring Caryl unless he brought Carson. Would Carson come? He would.

24

"Mrs. Oakfield, Mr. Bleeker, Carson Bleeker," Lieutenant Sims said.

The two adults nodded. Carson stared through the woman.

"Mrs. Oakfield, Mr. Bleeker has agreed to listen to what you have to say. In fairness to you, I think you should know that Carson's prejudice against the House of Logran comes directly from his father, from what he learned of the Organization's research some five or six years ago."

"Thank you, Lieutenant. Would you ask Tallie to bring Andy in, please?"

"Certainly." The lieutenant did not salute, but the effect was the same.

No one spoke until Tallie came in shepherding a running toddler who climbed up on Mrs. Oakfield's lap.

Carson turned away. Tallie was a traitor to everything he had felt and wanted, *and still did* feel and want. He could not understand himself.

"Mr. Bleeker, my daughter, Otalie, whom Carson knows as Tallie."

Carson's father nodded. Tallie said, "Mr. Bleeker."

"The baby is my adopted son, Andrew Logran Spencer-Oakfield, the sole owner and titular head of the Logran Organization."

Mr. Bleeker stared.

"Hi," Andy said.

"Ah . . . hi," Mr. Bleeker replied.

"Hi, Carson," Andy said.

Carson said nothing.

"Mr. Bleeker, would you object to having both of your children present for this conference? After all, it is about their futures."

"No objection."

"Tallie, ask Caryl to come in, please."

"Of course." Tallie smiled at her mother and left the room.

"Carson, please join us here," the woman said.

Carson got out of the chair he had chosen as the farthest-away he could sit. He walked over and sat in the chair by his father.

Caryl came in. She stood by the door for a minute. "Daddy, if I come kiss you, will you let me go?"

Daffyd Bleeker looked as if she had gutted him.

"Yes, Caryl," he said.

Caryl ran over and threw herself into his arms.

In a minute, she pulled away, ran around the table, and sat in the chair next to Mrs. Oakfield. Andy held out his arms to her, and Caryl looked up at his mother. "Oh, Aunt Persis!" she cried. "He wants to come to me. May I hold him?"

Mrs. Oakfield chuckled. "Of course, Caryl. He won't break. Very sturdy baby." She plopped him down on Caryl's lap. "Just remember, when he wants to go somewhere else, he gets to."

Caryl nodded. "Of course."

Carson tried not to stare. The Caryl he'd known loathed babies and small children. People paid too much attention to them.

The mental picture of N'omi's round little dark face filled his mind, and he realized he was jealous. Andy was a little kid he'd like to hold. He gritted his teeth and returned his gaze to the tabletop.

Yes, Mrs. Oakfield explained. Mr. Bleeker's evaluation of the Logran Organization's former research was accurate. However, upon the death of the previous head of the Organization, all such studies had been canceled, all persons serving as experimental subjects had been generously compensated, and all programs had been completely voided. No experimentation of the kind previously carried out was or ever again would be conducted by the Logran Organization.

Carson heard the siren song of the woman's beautiful voice with almost as much shock as he had the first time— over the radio when he had crouched behind the house in the ghost town. He wanted to put his fingers in his ears, sing loudly, do anything to avoid listening. Her belief in the truth of what she said was so clear that he found himself wanting to believe it, too. He mustn't. Da knew what she represented—everything he and Carson both loathed. He must be strong! He must not give in.

"I sit on the Board of Directors of the Organization,"

Mrs. Oakfield went on, "as Andy's representative. The Board agreed to put the resources of the Organization behind the search for your children. But I also represent the House of Logran, a separate entity. The House, which Caryl wants so much to join, is a *school*. The students—they include all my children, natural and adopted, by the way—have two things in common: very high intelligence and psi characteristics. Together, with the best and most honorably committed of teachers and scientists, we are trying to find out what must be known about these special talents in order to insure full, happy, productive lives for all."

"Mommie," Andy said. He held out his arms to her. "It hurts."

Both male Bleekers stared. Caryl's gentle embrace couldn't possibly be hurting the child. And Caryl made no remonstrance.

"Will Randy do?" his mother asked Andy. "Mommie's busy."

Andy nodded. "Randy fine."

"Caryl, would you ask Randy to come get him, please?"

"Tallie's worried," Caryl said.

Mrs. Oakfield smiled ruefully. "Ask Tallie to ask Randy. I forget you've been with us so short a time."

Carson felt at sea. He heard perfectly normal, sensible words, but they made no sense.

Randy came in, caught up the baby, and put him on his shoulders. He smiled at everyone and went out. Andy crowed.

"Am I to take it that I have just seen a demonstration of telepathy?" Mr. Bleeker inquired.

Mrs. Oakfield nodded. "And empathy. I knew Carson was distressed, but . . ." She shook her head. "Later, perhaps. For now, we have other things to discuss."

218

Mr. Bleeker nodded. Carson's confusion simply deepened.

"Whether you believe me is your choice, Mr. Bleeker," Mrs. Oakfield said. "But before you decide not to, I suggest you do several things."

"And what are those?" Carson had never heard his father's voice so devoid of inflection.

"Use your connections in the business world as you did before. See what they have to report. We will supply you with any information you want or with the unedited sources of such data to examine personally. Ask anyone any question you wish. We have no concern about the answers. The truth can only help our cause."

Mr. Bleeker nodded. "That seems fair," he said.

"Second. Try to put aside your prejudices. Recognize that they are based upon the policies and practices of the former head of the Organization—who was, in our opinions, severely mentally ill."

She leaned forward. "I am not psi-talented, but I do not believe that this highly subjective method of operation is typical of you. I do believe that you find this whole situation particularly difficult because you are not acting—and reacting—in a characteristic manner. If this seems rude, I beg your pardon. But I do not withdraw the statements."

Mr. Bleeker shifted in his chair. He started to speak, then caught himself. Carson watched his father relax.

"I have never been told off so courteously before," Mr. Bleeker said. "And objectively, I must agree that you're right. I find myself . . . somewhat embarrassed both by my behavior and my attitude."

Mrs. Oakfield smiled—but only faintly, as if in comradely reaction.

"My third suggestion is that you come and visit us. Live at the House of Logran, perhaps as a visiting lecturer, for as long as you feel necessary. Examine, in person, the young people who are members of the House and who will one day be policy-makers of the Organization. Get to know all of us. See for yourself what our conversations, actions, and interactions tell you. Make a total evaluation.

"We have nothing to hide. If we did, you would find it. We all know that. Arrange to contact anyone you like, including the police, in any manner, on any schedule you determine. But *come!* See and judge for yourself."

"And while I'm doing it, what happens to my children?"

"Whatever you wish."

Caryl stiffened. "No! I want to stay!" She pleaded with her father. "Oh, Daddy, I'm so happy there. They're already teaching me how not to—to be so awful. They like me. Nobody ever has. I like them, too. Please, Daddy, let me stay!"

Daffyd Bleeker stood up and paced. "Caryl, I wish I could believe you are the one speaking. If you're drugged, hypnotized, or under some other kind of compulsion—if somebody's making you say that, Caryl, even if you think you really want to . . . It would be truly criminal—and I could never live with myself—if I did not take you away."

"Daddy, it's not like that at all! They're not some kind of cult or a bunch of brainwashers or—or Svengalis, or anything. *Really* they aren't. Mostly, they tell me I have to make up my own mind about things. I know you don't believe that, but it's true!"

"Suppose it wasn't, Caryl," Mrs. Oakfield said.

Both Carson and his father stared in disbelief, in incomprehension.

"Suppose the real you was down underneath *hating* every word your mouth was saying. Suppose we were what he fears, and you had only one hope of getting away from us. If your father didn't take you, you'd be enslaved forever.

Suppose it was like being back at the commune with Pastor whipping you. Wouldn't you want to be rescued?"

"But it's not like that!"

"I know that. All the others at the House know that. *You* know that. But *he doesn't.*"

Everyone considered her words.

"If we both promise you that you may come back when he has learned he can trust us, would you be willing to leave until then?"

Caryl rocked back and forth in the chair. Finally she looked up. "I won't be willing to, but I'll go. Where do you want to put me, Daddy?"

"I don't want to *put* you anywhere, Caryl," Mr. Bleeker said. "I want to take you home."

"I won't go. Not just like that, without any hope."

Mr. Bleeker paced again.

He stopped and looked across the table at the woman. "You win. I'll come to the House. Caryl will come with me. What she does, I do. Where she goes, I go." He paused. "I do not believe you can stop me from finding it out if what you are doing is wrong."

As if making the decision had taken all the steel out of his soul, he slumped into the chair. "God in heaven, woman. How I hope I am the one who is wrong."

"No!" Carson thrust himself out of the chair so hard that it fell over behind him. "Dad, you can't! You told Mother what they were, what they are! You said you'd commit her or divorce her, do awful things to us, if she even wrote a letter! You can't do this! It's not fair!"

Even to himself, in a small, objective part of his mind that evaluated what he was saying, Carson sounded as if he were younger than Caryl, as if he were again the little boy who heard Daddy say terrible things to Mother.

Mr. Bleeker looked up at his son. "No, Carson, it is *not*

fair. It is necessary. I was right then, and Mrs. Oakfield agrees that I was. To keep you safe, I would have done what I least wanted to do. If what I learned then is still true, I shall find it out. If the House of Logran is what she says it is, and what Caryl believes it to be, then it is what your mother and I have looked for for nearly fourteen years, the right place for you both."

Carson stormed. "I can't go. I won't!"

"Mr. Bleeker, does Carson have any other place to go?" Mrs. Oakfield asked.

Slowly, the man nodded. "He has."

"I'll go anywhere, anywhere to get away from all of you!"

"There is a man named Ed," Mr. Bleeker said. "I do not know him, but Carson does. I believe he could go to Ed."

Carson's world solidified. Yes, he could go to Ed. He would, and he'd never come back.

He wouldn't tell them that. He'd just go. He picked up the chair and sat in it. "How soon can I go?"

"As soon as I can arrange it," Mr. Bleeker said.

"If I may?" Mrs. Oakfield raised her eyebrows.

Mr. Bleeker nodded.

"At once," Mrs. Oakfield said. "Caryl, will you ask Paul to come in, please?"

Caryl nodded and smiled.

Paul came in, and Carson looked at the tabletop.

"Take him to Ed, please, dear," Mrs. Oakfield said. "Right now."

"Thank God," Paul said. "I'll need help."

Mrs. Oakfield leaned back in her chair and smiled up at her tall son. "How about Basil?"

Paul smirked. "He's thrilled."

He turned to Carson. "Come out to the field in about fifteen minutes. It'll take us that long to put a pack together for you. And don't give me any infantile nonsense about

222

how you won't take anything of ours. You'll take it or I'll follow you and drop it." He strode out.

Carson refused to say good-bye to his father or Caryl. He got into the helicopter and slumped into a seat. "Why did you have to come?" he growled at Basil. "One of you is too many."

Basil looked at him with an expression so . . . so clinical that Carson felt like a virus under an electron microscope.

"You are a very powerful empathic sender," Basil said in exactly the tone of voice he might have said, "You are a thirteen-year-old boy."

"What you feel, every empath around you feels," he continued. "Your pain and anger are so great that Andy, who received it, was in acute pain. Mrs. Oakfield, Randy, Tallie to some extent, and I are the . . . call it filters. Some characteristic we have—about which we don't know much, yet—screens out the emotional content and lets receivers function on an intellectual level. That's why I sound like a robot. No feelings. Alone with you in your present regressive state, Paul would have to drug you or knock you out—which he could and would do, if necessary—in order to be able to function."

"What the hell's that supposed to mean?"

"Oh, use your mind," Paul snapped. "Presumably, you have one. Though I'm beginning to doubt it."

Basil spoke before Carson could get out his angry rejoinder. "Hold it, Paul. I'll tighten up," he said.

The strained, set look of controlled anger on Paul's face smoothed out. He nodded and smiled at Basil, then spoke to his passenger. "Sorry, Carson. Reaction, not intention."

Carson was totally confused. He didn't understand one word of what was being said—not even what he'd said. He retreated into silence.

Paul did not give away the location of Ed's cabin by

flying too near it. He chose to land at a place from which Carson could make his own way with a map they gave him. Take him a day and a half, he estimated, but they'd provided him with plenty of water and enough trail food for three days. If Ed had already moved on to the ghost town, Carson could fill up the canteen at the well and follow him.

No one said one word when the copter landed. Carson and Basil got out. Basil helped Carson into the backpack as if he were loading a mule, got back into the copter, and shut the door. Carson hiked away, not looking back. Paul waited until Carson was out of range of the dust and debris the rotors would kick up, then took off.

Ed sat on the steps, looking down the trail. Carson slogged up, unbelted and dropped his pack, and practically fell onto the step beside the old man.

"What did you do?" Ed greeted him. "Walk away from your own wake?"

"I feel like it," Carson said.

25

The short days and long, cold nights of the desert winter and early spring passed slowly for Carson, a slowness he hugged to himself as insulation against the pain of remembering. He did not realize for how long he refused to think, to feel emotion, but Ed did. Being Ed, he neither said nor did anything to change Carson, but let him come out of it himself.

After the authorities had dug away the rockfall and exhumed the stolen goods, money, and weapons from the old mine, the two of them moved to the ghost town. They rebuilt the best of the remaining houses into a tight, weather-sealed home. On an irregular basis, Ed went to Jackson or to Rightway to purchase or pick up much of the material and supplies they needed. Carson stayed in the valley.

Little by little, Carson realized that he had one thing he must do. He didn't want to, because he wanted to stay here, isolate, never again to allow himself either to grow up too fast or to drop into childhood with such pain and suddenness. At last his need to do it prodded him into memories, into thought, into emotion. Perhaps if he got it over with, he could forget again.

"Ed," he said one evening at supper, "I've got to go see my mother."

Ed nodded. "Wondered when you'd come to doing that thing," he said. "Where is she?"

Carson told him.

"Long way. Well, best do it tomorrow. We'll start down at daybreak. The telephone people finally got around to fixing that line. You can call from the station."

"Call?"

"Your father. For ticket money."

Carson decided not to go.

Three days later, he hiked down alone. Using Ed's station key, given to the old man by the Followers, he opened the door.

He called the office. His father's secretary arranged for rail and flight tickets and to telegraph money, all of which he could pick up at Coltburg, the next station to the south. She would send enough money for him to get some new clothes, stay overnight at a hotel, and take a taxi to and from the hospital. He took the first southbound train, purchasing a ticket to Coltburg on board with money Ed had lent him.

Carson had learned how to function without either thinking deeply or feeling much of anything, and practiced both. If he let himself think, he would remember Mother. She'd been so pretty. In the year or so before she'd gone to the hospital, she'd stopped being quite so attractive, but if she was getting well, she . . .

Carson found her absolutely beautiful, groomed and garbed as he remembered her being when company came. The hospital resembled none he had ever seen before, being much more like a luxurious hotel, with small cottages around the central building and extensive landscaping. Nobody wore uniforms. Even the doctors and nurses and therapists were in street clothes, distinguishable from patients and visitors only by unobtrusive badges. His semiconcern about visiting in a place where people were sick disappeared in moments.

His mother was overjoyed to see him. How was he? What had he been doing? Where did they live now? Did he like the house better than he had the old one? Where was he going to school? Let's see, he'd be in seventh grade this year, wouldn't he? My, he'd grown and put on muscles!

She asked, then answered most of her own questions. Carson, who needed to talk, found she needed him to listen. He wondered, flooded in her words, if she had ever listened to him. Perhaps when she was over her first exuberance, she'd be interested in what he had to say. Carson remained in the city an extra day and went back to the hospital. All that day, Elisha talked about her life there. She had been discharged twice, relapsed, and come back. This time, she—and her therapists—thought she'd make it. She told him the life history of every person at the establishment—though how she could have learned about them, he couldn't imagine, if she never listened to anyone. Was it only he to whom she did not wish to listen? Why?

Not once in the two days did Elisha mention Caryl's

name. On the one occasion when Carson, desperate, tried to tell his mother about Caryl and where she was and why, Elisha changed the subject halfway through one of his sentences.

He left, making an empty promise to come to see her again soon.

He cashed in his airline ticket and took the train all the way back upstate. The train cost less, took longer, and once he was on, he didn't have to get off until he was there.

Carson sat, staring out the window, wrapped in intentional isolation, and *thought* for a whole day. His desolate disappointment almost solidified the nothingness into which he had thrust himself. If the sound of the wheels over the rail-joints hadn't turned into one phrase, repeated over and over, "Like mother, like son, like mother, like son, like mother, like son," the disappointment probably would have won. He *would not* allow himself to become like Elisha.

An imperative as real as Ed, as necessary as breath, stared at him from the reflection of his eyes in the window. His time of decision had come. If he would not accept his mother's way, he must accept another. Not hiding, even if it was to be with Ed. Hiding solved nothing. It was like running away and staying away. The time had come to face himself, actually to do the growing up his father said he'd done.

Carson had assumed his inability to exist any longer in a vacuum was caused by his need to see his mother, and in a way, it had been. He did have to face that reality, but doing so could have come later. His misery was only the reaction to accepting what he already knew. More important, he had done it to put off—again—accepting the realities of the present free of his childhood reactions and beliefs.

228

Mother wasn't what he'd always wanted her to be, what he'd told himself she was until Caryl came. Quite probably, she never had been. That knowledge didn't keep him from loving her, but it did make a little less painful the fact that she did not love him—or, he corrected, she didn't love him the way he wanted her to.

Da did. He always would. Enough to let his son leave him again despite his desire—and promise—to be a regular part-time father, a promise Carson had made it impossible for him to keep.

Caryl did, too. Enough to go through the hell of confession and what Carson now realized was her almost impossibly difficult effort to show him she'd changed.

He loved them both. He'd always loved them. The answer to the question Ed had said Caryl mightn't ask him was so simple he hadn't realized it. In one way, he'd been more mature than either of his parents. Somebody had to love Caryl. It wasn't fair that nobody did. He hadn't liked her—nobody could have—but he loved her, exactly as he'd always wanted Mother to love him.

If what he knew intuitively and empathically to be true proved out, the House of Logran was exactly what Da had said: the right place for him. They'd offered. Not in so many words, but for what other reason could Paul and Tallie and Randy and Basil have met them in the desert? To *show* him.

He crossed his arms against the bottom of the window and put his head down on them. He could no longer face his own image.

He did not know when he went to sleep, but he woke when the train stopped. He glanced up.

The blurred reflection might have been his father's face, so much did they look alike. The same eyes looked back as he'd seen when Da had said he still had his paying to do—but Carson could have nine errors of judgment free.

Wrong, Carson said to himself.

He grinned, and the reflection cleared. He looked into his own eyes and made his decision. "Da and Caryl and the House," he said aloud. "Pay them for my mistakes. No! *Show them.* Start again—free and clear."

The sun came out. Quite literally, Carson felt as if he were responsible for its reappearance in a sky dull gray since he'd left Ed's and—though blue as only desert skies can be throughout the winter—dull gray in his remembrance. Everything had been dull gray for weeks.

But it wasn't! Not now. Not anymore.

He tossed his luggage off the train at Rightway Station, jumped down after it, and waved good-bye to the conductor. He reached for the key before he realized the station was open. He gawked.

Was it Friday? Couldn't be. *Then why . . . ?*

Go ask, dope! he told himself.

Carson strolled over to the ticket window. Even if the person there was a Follower, Pastor wasn't around to make the people capture and enslave him again. And Carson was older, stronger, and warned. He almost wished somebody'd start something.

"How come the station's open on a Wednesday?" he asked the woman in the little office.

"Oh, it has been for three months," she said. "Mondays, Wednesdays, and Fridays. Hey, don't I know you?"

Carson debated, then said a mental *To hell with it,* and answered. "Oh, yes, I'm the kid your pastor sent out with those guys to be killed. Didn't work, I'm happy to say."

The woman leaned forward. "Oh, Carson! I be so glad! None of us wanted that. We know now what happened to us. A good thing got twisted and spoiled by a bad man. Be Caryl all right?"

"She was the last time I saw her," Carson replied, trying to give the impression that he'd seen her two days ago.

"Be she—be she better?"

"If you mean has she killed off her telekinesis, the answer's no. If you mean is she learning to use it, and her telepathy and empathy and other talents—for the right reasons—the answer's yes."

The woman drew away from him a little. Carson followed up his attack with a change of subject. "Why did you decide to open the station three days a week?"

She leaned toward him again, eager. "We found out all sorts of things after—after Pastor's Farewell Ceremony. The Followers own this whole area! We called in the county geologists and found out there be enough groundwater right around the station to supply a small community. People need places to live since the earthquake. Businesses and factories have to be relocated. Jackson's getting three new ones, and it be only forty minutes away by train. We're going to build the kind of city here that we believe in and lease homes to people who'll take care of the land as we do. We got together, all of us, and decided not to wait for After the End. We can do something positive now."

"Solar and wind energy, water recycling, everybody with enough ground to grow their own vegetables, maybe raise chickens and rabbits?" Carson hazarded.

She nodded vehemently. "Some of us from the Community will be the first residents. We'll set examples, try to show the new people how to live in harmony with the land and Follow The Way. Matthew and I and our children have been selected."

Carson had her name now. She was the wife of the

schoolteacher—and had been expecting a baby the last time he saw her.

"Gee, Betty, that's great. Boy or girl?"

She smiled. "Boy. Little Matthew."

"Big Matthew will teach in the school here?"

"And I'll open a child-care center." She smiled at him with a semi-sly twinkle. "As the twig be bent, so grows the tree."

Carson laughed. He'd always liked the *people* at the commune. He hoped they prospered and succeeded. What could he remember from *The Book of The Way* that would be appropriate? " 'May the Lord show the light of His countenance upon thee, and in that light, may thee and thine grow strong and clean.' "

Betty smiled. "Do we have our first convert—by choice?"

Surprised, Carson laughed. He felt no merriment. "No way. I felt like a prisoner. Don't ever do that to anybody again, or you'll fail."

Betty's face, animated during their conversation, smoothed into the almost-mask the Followers wore so often. "We have learned that lesson well, Carson."

He didn't know what more to say. "Well, I've got to change. Can't go back into the hills in my city clothes."

"Be our guest. There be running water and a real toilet in the rest room."

Carson had discarded every item of clothing—he'd outgrown everything including the boots—when he bought his city clothes to visit Mother. The money from Da had been enough to buy four sets of everything he'd wear in the mountains, and gifts for Ed. He'd been ready to send back all but ticket money, but had remembered Paul's words—"infantile nonsense about not taking anything from us." He put on new underwear, jeans, and a wool shirt, two pairs of socks, and his new boots. *Hope I'm not chafed and blistered by the time I get there,* he thought.

When he emerged from the rest room, Betty called to him. "Carson?"

He went over to the window.

"Come to visit us, when next Ed does," she said softly, the mask back in place. "It do be . . . all right. Thee may go whenever thee wishes. We love and care about thee, and always did, although we—we treated thee wrongly. Thee and thy sister be always welcome."

Carson was sufficiently surprised that he almost blurted out he'd rather go directly to hell without passing Go, but he clamped his teeth together. "I do not think I can do that yet," he said instead. "When I can, I shall come."

Betty had a pretty smile. "I shall tell the others," she said. "We do not expect thee to forget, but we hope, one day, thee can forgive."

Carson looked at her for a long moment. "I'm learning to do that, about a lot of things," he said.

Betty looked down.

"It wasn't all bad," Carson said. "I learned a lot. And . . ." How could he say it right? "I do not want to forget my *friends* in —" he still couldn't say "Rightway" without making it into a curse—"in the Community. Say greetings to them for me."

"I will do that," she answered. "Go in peace."

"Peace be with thee," Carson responded as automatically as he would have months ago. He waved once as he started back to Ed's.

Peace, indeed. He hadn't even had to relive all of it to have everything fall into place. Why?

Caryl had told him once, and he'd ignored it. "Believe what you feel, not what you think."

He wasn't a telepath, but he *was* an empath. "A thousand times better than I am," she'd said.

Pain came with his remembrance of how he'd denied, shut away, disbelieved, even hated, one of the most precious memories of his life: Tallie and Paul and Basil and Randy—and Caryl and Ed—that night in the desert by the spring.

He turned back to look at the beginning of his life here, at the tiny station standing as the only outpost of civilization, linked to the rest of life by two shining rails and a single line of wire strung between telephone poles. He remembered something he'd done then—something that had never passed through his mind in all the months and months. When he first got here, he'd buried three dollars and fifty-five cents in coins. He laughed. Let some lucky builder find it. They'd wonder, but they'd never find out.

He took less than a dozen steps before he turned back.

Carson needed no landmarks. With the luck, he located the plastic sack of coins. Jingling the money, he went back to the station.

He called his father's office.

"He's still at the House of Logran," Marilyn said.

"What's the number?"

She told him.

He called the House of Logran collect. His father answered.

Carson sang all the way back to Ed's. His voice didn't break once, and he was going to be a tenor—a real Welsh tenor! Oh, glory!

He told Ed about his trip, about what he had learned by visiting his mother, about his talk with Betty, but going

234

over all the details was no longer something he needed to do. He had himself and his past and, he hoped, his present and future under control.

Ed listened, nodded, and dug into his leather money pouch. Silently, he handed Carson a folded, somewhat dirty piece of lined newsprint. Like the school notebook paper at Rightway . . .

And now the word was just a place-name.

Carson unfolded it slowly. The message he wrote that night he had seen the car lights speeding toward Rightway stared up at him, dim and smeared.

"I have carried that for all this time," Ed said slowly. "For all this time, I did not know whether I had done rightly. I believe, now, that I did."

Carson nodded, still looking at the paper. Very slowly indeed, he tore the paper into tiny scraps. He held them up. The slight breeze scattered them across the sands. He could not see one. Yes, Ed had the patience, the understanding, the knowledge of people—of him—to let him make his own way out of his troubles, to meet his parents again when he needed to, for his own reasons. Carson could never say his thanks, or even show it.

"I wish you really were my gramps," he said.

"I would be honored if you called me that," Ed said. "I never had anyone who did."

26

When the copter dropped into the valley, Ed and Carson were ready. Stubborn was spending a week or so in Rightway, and the cabin was as secure as they could make it.

Tallie had come with Paul, and her sense of hopeful anticipation made Carson laugh with delight. She piled out of the cabin before the rotor stopped and ran to him, bent over with the force of the wind.

Carson caught her. She threw her arms around him. He hugged her hard. They both laughed.

"Gramps," Carson said, turning to his most important person, "this is my friend Tallie." Ed knew almost as much about Tallie as he did, but Carson had to say it, to make clear—to himself?—the relationship.

Ed's eyes twinkled at her, but his voice was solemn. "It is in my mind that we have met before," he said, sounding as Welsh as Caernarfon.

Tallie stared at the old man. Her expression changed. "Hi, Gramps," she said. "I'm so glad you waited for us."

Ed chuckled. "Can't get rid of me that easy, lass," he said. "In our family, we live almost forever."

"I've never had a gramps," Tallie said softly. "May I adopt you?"

Ed bowed.

Carson stared.

"To be a member of your family is honor," Ed said, "even though you are of the English. That is a problem, but I shall think on it."

Tallie snickered.

Paul joined them and put his arm around Carson's shoulder as if Carson were . . . his brother? That's the way it felt.

Ed, with his usual sense of the real, the present, broke the spell.

"Do you intend to let that devil's machine sit there on idle for the rest of the day, or shall we all enter it and be borne elsewhere?"

"Elsewhere, Gramps," Paul said.

"Somebody else came with us," Tallie said as they carried the few things Carson and Ed had decided to take with them to the copter.

Andy's laugh greeted Carson as he opened the door.

"Carson's happy!" Andy announced.

The little boy was securely buckled into a car-seat, so Carson couldn't pick him up, but he tossed his pack into the back without noticing where it went and snuggled the delighted toddler.

"Yes," he said. "Carson's happy."

"Andy's happy, too," Andy said.

Why it was so important to him that Andy had come, that Andy was happy, Carson didn't know, but he no longer felt confused. He felt good and accepted and accepting—and had his answer. Andy knew he'd showed them, all of them.

"Hi, Gramps," Andy said.

Carson turned.

Ed's eyes, twinkling in the way Carson knew signaled his most cheerful moments, observed the gleeful youngster in the car-seat. "And who are you, young man?" he asked.

"Andrew Donald Logran Spencer-Oakfield," Andy said proudly.

"Sole owner and titular head of the Logran Organization," Carson quoted.

"And most important person in the House of Logran," Tallie added.

"Now that," Ed said, "is a most positive beginning to this matter."

Carson gave Ed a boost into the copter and ran around to get in the opposite door. As he buckled himself in, he heard Andy laugh again.

"Gramps happy," Andy said.

"Yes, lad," Ed agreed. "Gramps happy, too."

The copter set down on a grassy meadow. "Well done, young man," Ed said. "With you at the controls, it is possible that this infernal machine may be on the side of the angels."

Paul smiled broadly and attempted to bow.

Tallie turned to Carson and Ed in the backseat. "Andy

and I'll go put her away with Paul. Somebody's waiting for you. We'll bring in your packs."

Carson helped Ed out. The long drop to the ground was not easy for the old man. Quite suddenly Carson was infused with the realization of how much he would, one day not long enough from now, miss this man. He said nothing, but he knew Tallie and Paul—and Andy—sensed this with him and mourned as deeply.

Daffyd Bleeker stood waiting at the edge of trees that bordered the southern end of the meadow. Carson and Ed walked over to him.

"Hello, Da," Carson greeted him. "I'm back for good." He stepped into and returned a hearty hug.

"This is Ed," Carson introduced. "He said once that Caryl and I were his grandkids, and I think it may almost be true. Ed, my father, Daffyd Bleeker."

The two men shook hands.

Carson stared. In all the time he had spent with Ed, he had never realized that his father and the old man were much alike physically. The same solid, stocky body, the same short neck, the same way of walking, the same alert awareness of everything going on around them. Ed's long hair, full beard, shaggy mustache, and shaggier eyebrows disguised any facial resemblance he might have to the younger man. But how, Carson wondered, could he have failed to recognize the most obvious sign of all?

Mr. Bleeker looked down at the clasped hands. "I do not doubt that we are related." He sounded very Welsh. "See?"

The two men spread their hands and held them next to one another.

"Carson, do you the same," Ed directed.

But for the difference in age and the signs of life and

work, the hands were identical. Three generations of one family.

"Is . . ." Carson swallowed and started again. "Is the last name you lost so long ago *Bleeker?*"

Old Ed nodded. "I thought yours sound familiar when I first heard it," he said.

The three of them stood there, smiling identical smiles—except for age and hairiness—at one another.

"Now then, our Daffyd," Old Ed said, "is it right here for the lad? Is this the exception to *The Rule?*"

Daffyd Bleeker nodded, his face absolutely without hint of humor. "Much as it goes against the grain," he said, "I have learned here that once in ten generations or so, one has good reason to trust the English."

Slowly, Ed turned his shaggy head from side to side. He let out his breath with a "Wheeeeew."

"Lead on, son of my uncle's son's son, or whoever it is that you are," he said. "Let us see if I can feel the same."

You will, Carson thought.

He knew Ed would. He already did.

Epilogue

One lovely summer morning, Carson and Ed sat on a log beneath a tree, not talking much, just being together. *Forever* had become *soon* for Ed, a fact he welcomed with complete composure. Carson, too, had learned to accept it, glad, now the time had come, that they were together.

The old, old man, nearly ninety—or considering his lack of concern about the number of years he had lived, perhaps nearer one hundred—reached into his pocket.

"The time has come to pass the luck," he said.

Carson, moist-eyed but tearless, as were both of Daffyd's children—their unusually large tear ducts pouring the tears down into the nose and throat—turned to him slowly.

"I said once that when the time came, I would be here," he said very clearly.

Ed opened his hand. On the scarred, rough palm lay a thick, flat circle of solid gold, the stamping long since worn away.

Carson clasped Ed's hand between both of his.

"Go, now, son of my brother's son's son," Ed said. "I must be alone, to make my last peace."

"Not alone," Carson said.

"Death is not . . . good to remember," Ed said very softly indeed.

"Nor is life, sometimes," Carson told him, "but it's always better with someone you love."

Ed sighed. "I always wished I had been there," he said, "to hold his hand."

Carson nodded.

"God bless you, and good luck." Ed spoke the words quietly but clearly.

The clasped hands rotated a half-turn.

"When your turn comes to pass the luck," Ed whispered, "may you be so blessed."

Forever became *now,* and Carson sat and held Ed's hand for a long, long time.